Reluctant Heir

by

Barbara Jean Miller

The Wild Rose Press, Inc.
PO Box 708
Adams Basin, NY 14410-0708
Visit us at www.thewildrosepress.com

Publishing History
First Edition, 2024
Trade Paperback ISBN 978-1-5092-5497-2
Digital ISBN 978-1-5092-5498-9

Published in the United States of America

Dedication

For our gaming friends, Rose and Gary

Chapter One

Gerard Cochran blotted his bloody nose with his handkerchief as he sprinted down the boulevard toward his father's lodgings, his booted feet sliding on the cobbles when he turned into their street. He stole a glance over one shoulder, then hesitated at the outside door. He had outrun his pursuers but saw a crippled old Frenchman and his servant sitting across the street at a table outside the café. Gerard did not know why he hesitated to show them where he lived. Just because he had seen them all over the northwest quarter of Paris did not mean they were following him or had any interest at all in him, the son of a British major posted to Paris after the war in the Peninsula. He ran up the stairs and flung open the door into the midsection of Tully, his father's wiry batman. The old fellow grabbed him by the arm and scrutinized his face.

"You have been fighting again."

"When attacked I have to defend myself."

"I told you not to tour the city with those drummer boys. They go out looking for trouble."

"But I have no other friends." Gerard went to the small chamber he occupied next to his father's bedroom. There was clean water in the pitcher, so he poured a basin full and took soap to his face and hands. One knuckle

1

was split, which would be hard to hide from his father. But it wasn't in him to back down from a fight. And these young French street thugs were no match for him and Crispin, a drummer from his father's brigade, unless they tackled them ten to one like today. Why they bothered to attack them he could not fathom. The English had won in the Peninsula. The war was over and the French had lost. Why couldn't they accept that?

While waiting for his father, Gerard convinced Tully to play chess with him on his father's folding chess board. The batman was an indifferent player and fell into every trap Gerard set for him. Winning so easily was not as satisfying as losing to his father, who was an excellent player, guarding every piece as jealously as Gerard did. Their matches of late often ended in stalemate.

When his father came in the door an hour later, Gerard slid his right hand onto his lap and picked up a pawn with his left. He had decided to risk another of his precious pawns to lure Tully into a trap, but the old man was being crafty today and hesitated. Gerard tried to ignore the critical blue gaze that swept over the board and then up and down his clothes.

Major John Cochran of the Horse Artillery cleared his throat. "Gerard, I've spoken to you about your reprehensible sense of humor before."

"What?"

"I see no less than two unsprung traps. You have two ways to win and yet you lure Tully out again."

"I knew it. 'Tis the last time I play with you." The old man whisked the pieces off the board and put them away.

"But I like the game to continue."

"Been fighting again, have you?" his father asked as

he tossed his cane and gloves on a chair.

Gerard felt his jaw drop and heard Tully guffaw.

"How did you know?"

"You are far too clean and tidy for this time of day." His father was stripping off his neckcloth and walked into his bedchamber to get out a fresh one. "I dine with Captain Scott this evening," he called from the other room. "Do you want to accompany me?"

It sounded more like an order than a request to Gerard. "Yes, but why? You never ask me to dinner with the officers."

His father came back in, tying his fresh neckcloth. "His brother teaches at a school in England. He might persuade him to put in a good word for you, if you don't turn up like a grub worm."

Major Cochran carried a cane now, though he had no need of one since his leg had healed. Gerard knew it was a sword stick and that a weapon of some sort was part of his father's identity even though, like most British officers, he favored civilian clothes when not in battle.

"What use is school unless they teach about artillery or strategy and tactics?"

"I'm sure they teach nothing of the sort. You will learn Latin and Greek and a great deal of law. Now, are you coming?"

"Yes, sir." Gerard failed to keep the disappointment out of his voice. He followed his father down the stairs and walked beside him along the crowded streets toward the Seine.

"Why do I have to go to school?"

"The war is over. It's time we gave some thought to your future."

"I thought to become a soldier like you."

His father glanced at him. "It's a profession without much of a future in wartime. Certainly none at all now that there is peace."

"You have done all right."

"But now that peace is made, I'll go on half pay. The grateful country won't show much appreciation once all the soldiers arrive back home with no jobs. The civilian population ever fears a standing army."

"It's not fair."

"Nothing is. That's why I want you to go into law. Perhaps you can right a few wrongs."

"I meant about the way soldiers are treated in their own country. Do you mean to go to England?"

His father shook his head. "I have a chance at a diplomatic post. If I get it, I will sell out. No more killing to make a living."

"But I could go with you." He still had to look up to his father, who was a few inches taller. At nearly eighteen Gerard held out no hope of catching up to him in height.

"If I don't get it I will have to go where I am posted."

"I would never care."

"No, you regard it as a high treat to be cold, wet and hungry the better part of the time."

"I never complained."

His father stopped to look at him and Gerard saw something different about his eyes, not just tiredness and resignation. That was always there. But pain, beyond what a wound would cause. "Isn't it enough that your mother died on campaign? Let me try to make a place for you in the world. I don't want you to turn out like me."

"But you're a hero and I admire you. Everyone does."

"When I was your age I took a wrong turn. I won't

let you do the same."

Gerard said nothing but followed when his father walked on, trying to savor these minutes since he suspected there would be precious few of them left.

"It isn't that I don't want you with me. But being in Paris makes me realize how much time has passed, how much I have lost."

"Mother came from Paris."

"Yes, so it is not a place I relish."

They had just come down the Rue Royale when Gerard saw the old lame Frenchman and his giant of a servant near the middle of the Place de la Concorde. His father stiffened and stopped, regarding the man with an intense expression. The gentleman hobbled up to them, leaning on a real cane of ebony wood and grasping the sleeve of his servant with the other hand for support.

"Major Cochran, I thought you might remember me." His voice was commanding and formal in spite of his infirmities. Gerard was startled by the man speaking English so fluently though his accent was heavy. Not Parisian but some other district.

"As well as you remember me," his father replied.

"So this is Gerard?"

"Yes, Gerard, this is General Soutine and his man Condé."

Gerard bowed formally and greeted the man in French, which caused raised eyebrows from both the Frenchmen.

Soutine smiled. "I see he has not forgotten everything his mother taught him. Major, I must speak with you privately. A moment only."

"Very well. Gerard, have Condé show you the obelisk. I need to talk with the general."

Gerard obediently went to the obelisk at the intersecting pathways and leaned against the base. He looked at the monument for his father's benefit but questioned the servant about where Soutine had fought and got a catalogue of battles that ended with Moscow, which had meant the end of many a career and very many lives. But it was a different theater of the war from the one where Gerard's father had fought. That plus the age difference convinced Gerard that his father and Soutine had never faced each other in battle. How then were they acquainted?

Condé was a giant of a man, with a speech impediment that caused him to lose the fronts of words. Gerard suspected it had to do with hearing loss, but once he had caught on to the problem he could understand him easily enough. Since Condé was a man of few words, Gerard spent his attention trying to catch what his father was saying to General Soutine. He picked up a garbled phrase here and there but nothing that made sense. Soutine wanted something from his father and he refused adamantly. It was not uncommon for officers on opposite sides to know each other and even develop a grudging respect. If Soutine's request could be granted, why not?

When his father broke off conversation with Soutine he bowed curtly, hardly more than a nod, and strode toward Gerard, commanding him to follow him.

"Condé says Soutine fought at Wagram. Isn't that where your father fought?"

"One of many places. What else did he tell you?"

"Nothing." Gerard picked up his pace to keep up with his father's long stride. "How do you know General Soutine?"

"It does not matter. He is an enemy of your

grandfather."

"Being on the other side that goes without saying, but it must have been decades ago. And since you are not on terms with your father, does it matter?"

"Let it rest, Gerard. Some wounds never heal."

"What did Soutine want?"

"Nothing he can have." His father paused and rested his hand on his cane head. "Are you done with questions for today?"

Gerard resumed his customary silence. There were so many things he was never permitted to ask about, especially his father's people in England. Gerard had the feeling his father had been disinherited for marrying a Frenchwoman, but he would have cut his tongue out rather than broach that subject.

Before they got to the café, his father threw his arm around Gerard's shoulder. "Forgive me for being so curt. You mean everything to me. It's just Paris that drags me down."

"General Soutine seems sad as well."

"He should stand as a lesson to both of us. That's what soldiering gets you if you're lucky, a limping existence in a city where no one cares about you. I wish I was done with the army."

"You only say that because the war is over. If there was another and you heard the call to arms, I think you would go."

His father stopped and looked down at him, shook his head, then smiled sadly. His lips curled up at the corners and his chiseled chin stood out sharply defined against his white stock. "I fear you are right."

Everyone told Gerard he looked like his father, but he wasn't as tall or as handsome. And he was nowhere near as self-assured. But it appeared that some of that command stance was an act. Still, his father was a hero no matter what he said. Gerard would trade all the comforts in the world to stay with him. How to convince him of this was the problem.

****

Northamptonshire, England, March 1815

Juliet Chandler hesitated outside her great-uncle's oaken study door before she knocked. She didn't like to eavesdrop, but it never hurt to assess the climate before entering a room where you were likely to be blasted by the frosty bite of the old man's tongue. The voices of her brother Charles reasoning with their great-uncle, retired General Alfred Cochran, told her nothing today as she smoothed the creases from her green morning dress and finger-combed her long blonde hair before she rapped.

"What is it?" the general's harsh voice demanded.

Juliet opened the door and leaned against it as she closed it. "You asked for me?" She refused to concede that he had sent for her and she had come at his bidding. She made every bow to one of his demands seem voluntary. It did not give her much power, but it was a fiction that made life here at Old Stand bearable.

"Sit down then, girl."

As she slid into one of the wooden armchairs, her great-uncle turned toward Charles, who was leaning against the edge of the large desk.

"Well, is he coming home?" the general demanded of her brother, who was reading a letter with a look of dread. Charles was her hero. He was tall, blond and handsome like their father had been, and he had the same skill at smoothing the rumpled feelings of General Cochran.

He leaned sideways to get better light from the window and looked up finally. "No, your son is part of the occupation force. In other words, he is not at liberty to return."

The old man glared at him under craggy gray brows. "And when he is at liberty?"

"I think I should go to Paris to talk to him." Charles began folding the letter. "Surely when he fulfills his duty I can convince him to come home."

"Give me that."

Charles sighed and passed the missive to the general, who carried it to the light and then held it at arm's length as he squinted at the page.

"How colorful. 'Over his dead body.' If he stays much longer in the artillery that is exactly how he will return." The old man tossed the sheet onto his broad desk.

"But, sir, was it not you who sent him away? Perhaps a conciliatory note in your own hand would be more convincing than the pleading of a second cousin."

"That was decades ago. If he has a particle of sense he will sell out now as you instructed him."

"Perhaps if you wrote to him yourself he would truly believe you want him back."

"Grovel to that whelp? It would be too much like surrendering. Juliet will just have to marry Claude."

"No!" she said before she could weigh the consequences. She stood up but was still a head shorter than the general, who rounded on her with a glare.

"What do you mean, no?"

She resisted the urge to back away. "I dislike Claude. I could never marry him."

"You'll marry whom you're told to, or no one."

She weighed her answer as she looked the old man in the face. "No one seems a much better choice. Claude has always been mean and spiteful. Besides, if I were fool enough to marry your grandson, he would get his hands on my money and run through it within a year."

"Cousin Nash won't marry Juliet. He says her tongue bites like a whip." Charles winked at her but her great-uncle only stared.

"Nash is old enough to be my father," she protested. "He has no interest in me."

The general nodded, not the reaction she was expecting. Was he agreeing with her?

Charles stood and faced their great-uncle. "Even if your son John returns there is no assurance that he would marry a cousin to please you, and he is two years older than Nash, more than twice Juliet's age. Neither John, Nash, nor Claude are right for her."

Their uncle blew out a disgusted breath. "There is one other option."

"What?" Charles asked.

"John's son."

Juliet stared at him. "He has a son?"

"Yes, he would be of an age with you. After John, he is the next in line. We'll bring the son here and polish him up. Maybe he'll be more malleable than his father."

"But where is he?" Charles demanded.

"With the army, I suppose. Check the enlistments for John's regiment. Find out if a brat named Gerald—no, not Gerald. What the devil was his name?"

He selected a key from the ring he carried and opened a small drawer in his desk. A worn letter caused him to frown and walk toward the window, then squint as he held it out in front of him. "Gerard—damn French name. Find Gerard Cochran and bring him here."

"But will he come either?" Charles asked.

"If he does and agrees to marry Juliet, then you can marry your cousin Melanthe with my goodwill, but no one marries from this house until a succession is established. Now get busy with your letter writing, and get out, both of you."

The siblings exited the room and closed the door to lean backward on the oak barricade and blow out a mutual breath of relief.

"Why can't we just escape this place?" Juliet demanded as she strode beside her brother down the hall toward the library which Charles used as his office.

"I told you. By the terms of Father's will, I don't inherit until I'm of age. We could leave but we'd have no money."

"Having a fortune is just a bother. It's never done either one of us any good."

"But he treats us a sight better than any of his other relations. I'd hate to have to live here with no expectations. Come and help me compose the letter." Charles threw the library doors open and took a seat at the large table in the center, pulling a blotter and inkstand toward him.

Juliet pulled a chair up beside him. "Charles, if we don't get either one of them to come home, I'd be willing to marry Claude if it would make you happy."

He put a hand on her shoulder. "That you shall not. Sacrifice your future to buy my happiness? That would be stupid. If all else fails, we hold out 'til I come into my money. Then I shall be your guardian and you may do as you wish."

"When will that be?"

"Unfortunately, not 'til I am five and twenty, another four years."

Chapter Two

Brussels, June 18, 1815

Gerard realized he had been right. Three months after he had predicted his father would march off to war again, he watched him ride out of the square in Brussels where their regiment had formed up. Napoleon had escaped Elba and in a daring march across France had, against all reason, drawn the remnants of his old armies about him. The British, Dutch, and Prussian armies had gathered to fight him. In many ways it had been a race against time. The English had to try to get back troops they had shipped to America to fight in that war. Wellington was in charge, of course, but so many brave fighters from Peninsular days would not be here to help. And Gerard was still not one of them, not really.

There had been fighting on the sixteenth. On the seventeenth his father rode out in a pouring rain. Gerard waved as his father smiled and saluted, then shook his finger and gave him a stern look, a visual reminder that he was to stay in Brussels no matter what the news from the front. That would be hard.

No matter how much Gerard tried to heed his father, he found himself in the street saying goodbye to comrades, drummer boys much younger than him marching off to battle. He knew all the orders and signals. He should be going as well. The least he could do was drum for them, but he wasn't quite old enough to enlist.

Usually he could stomach staying behind, but this time it seemed different. His father had given Gerard all his money and papers he usually carried secreted in a belt. He'd done it carelessly, not as though dying in battle was a possibility. Gerard put the belt on under his shirt without even looking at the contents.

If anything happened to his father, Gerard was to contact Captain Scott and make arrangements for that school in England. His father also gave him the address for his grandfather's estate in Northamptonshire, yet did not tell him what to do with it. Surely he would not want Gerard to go there. Then it occurred to Gerard that they would have to be notified if his father was killed.

The waiting was horrible and he barely slept that night knowing the next day could be decisive. On the eighteenth, when the wounded began to straggle or be carted back into Brussels, the worry was excruciating. Gerard helped carry water and bandage wounds. These were simple enough tasks since he did not know the men, but he found a dozen soldiers from his father's brigade and none could tell him about his father.

Gerard figured that by the time the column of wounded tapered off he would either know his father was still on the field or was dead. He had been through this before, working behind the lines to help when he was feeling nothing but black despair alleviated almost cruelly by some report of his father's bravery.

But this was different. He wanted to do more. When he thought about it, what he felt competent at had nothing to do with being a soldier. He didn't want to kill. He wanted all this to end. If he could have his wish, he would like to become a surgeon's assistant, perhaps even a surgeon, someday. As he extracted a wood fragment from a soldier's leg and applied a tight linen bandage, he made a mental note to ask Captain Scott if this school where his brother taught could train someone for such a profession.

Finally, at two in the afternoon, he could stand it no longer. He hitched a ride on one of the wagons carrying shot and powder to the battlefield. The driver knew him and let him ride post on the leader since he was short a man. His father would be angry, but he was so often angry anyway.

It had occurred to Gerard that his father was not immortal, nor infallible either. Perhaps he was wounded somewhere and would be glad to have Gerard come with water and help him back to Brussels.

When they came down the road past Mont St. Jean, all was chaos. Wounded and dead men and horses lay everywhere. As Gerard helped unload the wagon, dropping supplies by each cannon crew, he thought the horses almost made him feel worse, since they were innocent victims. But if it came to that, so were the soldiers. Yes, they killed each other, but they had not made the war. This battle could be laid only at the door of Napoleon and his devoted army. Though Gerard had lost his wish to become a soldier, if he had Napoleon in his sights at this moment he would shoot him dead without compunction.

He helped load the wagon with wounded for the return trip. Why had their army no ambulance carriages as the Frenchman Larrey had designed for their opponent's army? He abhorred the thought that individual men meant so little. At least his father had cared about his men. He choked on a sob for thinking of his father in past tense.

When he came to the field where he'd been told his father's brigade had stood, he did not see a man or boy left alive. He dodged the shells that smacked into the muddy ground. Most of the soldiers able to move would be sheltering on the reverse slope until the cannonade was over.

He found the body of Crispin, their drummer and his friend. Gerard bit his lip and tenderly moved him to the shelter of an upended caisson, realizing this could be himself lying here dead if his father had granted his wish. He looked everywhere at every face. His father was not here, nor were the colors. That meant there was hope. Perhaps he was in another part of the field or was only wounded. Gerard picked up the drum and had started toward the swell in the ground when Captain Givens rode up. Not from his father's regiment, but perhaps he'd seen him.

"You're Cochran's son."

"Aye, sir. Have you seen him?"

"Not in hours. We need a drummer. Can you do it?"

Gerard said, "Aye, sir," without thinking and trotted at a quick march after the man's horse. His company was moving in to fill the breach in the line. The captain began shouting orders to him. *Assemble*. The enemy had left off with the cannon barrage and was about to send cavalry over again. Gerard started beating out the orders over the groaning of the wounded. *Form square*.

He was standing in an open space with a square of redcoated men forming to his left and one to his right. At the last possible moment he was to run to the cover of one of the squares of soldiers. But the longer he could keep drumming the better the men stood for the cavalry charge to come against them.

He saw the French cavalry and felt bad again for the horses. He felt the rumbling of their hooves as they began their charge, heard the sabers swinging like scythes, and wondered how he ever could have glorified this. He kept up a steady drumming, measuring the distance to the closest square and how long it would take him to get there running with the drum. But it did seem to him that the horsemen were riding straight for him.

At least one of them was. Silence the drummer and you cut at the heart of the unit. And he had no weapon. Except the drum. He waited as long as he could, but he would not be caught from behind by circling cavalry. He would not run. At the last second he flung off the strap and whirled the drum around his head into the horse's face.

This set the beast back on its heels, and because the hussar tried to turn it, the animal came over sideways on its rider. Gerard scrambled for the cavalryman's saber but it was pinned under the horse, and the man was in no position to put up a fight anyway. The pounding of hooves got his attention but too late. The circling cavalry rode over both him and the downed man, though the horses leaped the struggling beast even as the pinned hussar cursed in pain. A crack sounded, and pain shot through Gerard's head.

****

Northamptonshire, England, June 19, 1815

It was already late afternoon, and Charles had just ridden back from the village with the post. Juliet clenched her hands in her lap as their uncle opened the bundle of mail on his desk. Flipping through the stack, he finally came to a letter that he unsealed and held at arm's length to read. He blinked his eyes hard, then opened them and squinted. "This tells me of a battle in Belgium, with an outcome far from certain, at a place called Quatra Bras, a few days ago. Old Reingold writes from London with the first word anyone has heard yet."

She had never seen her great-uncle look so old and unhappy. "Who won?" Juliet asked.

"We won't know until he writes again, but casualties are heavy." He handed the letter to Charles, who scanned it eagerly.

"I should have gone to find them before the war ignited again." Charles dropped the paper on the desk and paced the study. "Now it may be too late."

General Cochran shook his head. "It was already too late when we had our discussion in March. If you recall, it was only a few days later that we heard Napoleon had escaped Elba and was marching across France. Who could have imagined all his old commanders would abandon the Royalist army to rejoin him? Certainly John would never have come home once he knew."

Charles looked worried. "He might at least have sent his son home."

She saw the old man squinting at a newspaper he was holding in front of him and realized why Charles now acted as scribe for him. She wondered who had done so before they came to live at Old Stand two years ago.

"I could be in London by tomorrow and take ship the next day."

"We have not heard their fate. The battle is not over. We will wait."

"For news from the War Office?" Charles demanded.

The general drew a magnifying glass out of the drawer and focused it on the page of the *Times*. "John has not written in a very long time, but he would write about something like this to set my mind at rest. He was disobedient, not cruel."

Her brother looked up. "And if he doesn't write?"

General Cochran dumped the newspaper on the desk and blinked. "Then we will have our answer soon enough from the casualty lists."

Juliet cleared her throat. "Charles, did you establish if Gerard had enlisted?"

"I don't know," said Charles. "There is no record of it. Though who knows what might get left unreported on the eve of war. It would seem extraordinary if he had not joined at his age and in his circumstances. I would have."

The general looked up with a sad smile on his face. "Charles, I fear you are too much like your father and might thrust yourself into harm's way for the sake of finding them." The general watched her brother pace. "I am forever grateful that you never went army mad and begged for a commission."

"Much good it would have done me."

The old man shook his head. "Perhaps that's why your father left your affairs in my hands."

Charles looked toward her and shook his head. "I have responsibilities here—my sister."

"Not to mention the wool mill. Still, I am glad you did not pester me for a commission."

It was at times like this she realized their uncle had a genuine regard for them. "I'll go with him," she said.

A crack of laughter was followed by a measuring look from the general. "I grant you can ride or think as well as any man, even John, but I don't want you thrust into danger as well."

"If one of them is wounded, I might be useful," she said, not in a pleading way. Whining never swayed her uncle, just statements of fact. She had nursed her young cousin Jack through a broken arm. And she was no stranger to caring for invalids, having taken care of their mother for a year after their father's death had broken her health.

Charles blew out a tired breath. "Once banking is regularized, I must go to Europe anyway to see about our wool contracts."

"We can hire an agent to do that," the general argued. "Don't you see? If I have lost a son and grandson, I don't want to put you two at risk as well."

"I want to see for myself," Charles insisted. "And I agree that Juliet could come with me once the war is over."

"Why the devil would you do that, take your sister into a war-torn country?"

Charles hesitated. "If either of them is alive, her appearance may argue for a marriage. She can be more convincing than I can."

General Cochran squinted at her and then really looked at her as though for the first time. "You may have a point there. Having known her when she was a whey-faced chit, I had not realized how beautiful she has grown. Nor how courageous."

Juliet flushed with both anger and embarrassment but did not get to give voice to her conflicting emotions before the man continued.

"Very well. If an accident were to befall me, the fate of Old Stand would be uncertain. I must establish who my heir is, and quickly." He turned and stared out the back window as he spoke. "Besides your own man, take the head groom and that new footman, Gordon, with you. He's a veteran. You should be safe enough."

Charles edged toward the door as though he thought this permission might be rescinded. "We shall be victorious again."

The general nodded. "I admire your optimism about our chances, but believe me, the fate of the war is far from decided."

Charles blew out a tired breath. "I believe we will win. This was just a last desperate gasp by that madman Napoleon."

General Cochran stared out the window again. "Sometimes I think all those who go to war are mad and the maddest are the ones who do succeed. What say you, Juliet?" He turned to her. "Do you agree to marry an heir, either of them, if they should be found alive and sane?"

She realized for the first time that he was giving her a choice, a real choice. "There is no one else I wish to marry. If I did not entertain that possibility, I would not be willing to go."

He laughed less bitterly this time. "I never get a straight answer from you. I am used to hearing 'Yes, sir.' "

She smiled as though to a doddering old man. "You must be recollecting when you were in the army and your men had no choice but to obey you. Armies cannot work any other way."

"Certainly it's not a place for creative thinking even if you are mad. When we have word the war is certainly over, go then, but mind you come back safe even if you can't find the errant Cochrans. I know you are only going because Charles is and you don't want anything to happen to him."

As always he floored her with his departing shot, and she left the office admitting to herself that *was* why she wanted to go. If they found John and Gerard that would be wonderful, but she would not marry either of them unless she truly wanted to. And now she doubted the general would force her to. Moreover, he trusted her to keep her head over the slight inconvenience of travel over bad roads. Perhaps it was because of all those times he had stopped in her mother's sick room and found her on duty that he now trusted her like an adult.

****

Waterloo Field, June 19, 1815

His name being called penetrated Gerard's fogged brain. He lurched up on hands and knees and a spin of dizziness knocked him back down. More carefully, now, he staggered to his feet and looked around. There were soldiers moving about in the fog and some civilians tending the wounded or perhaps robbing the dead. His clothes were wet with either dew or rain.

The hussar and his horse were missing so must have survived. Odd that the man had not cut his throat. One hardly looked for mercy in the heat of battle. When he put a hand to his throbbing head, he recoiled on touching the gash at his hairline and staggered. Perhaps the cavalry man had thought him already dead.

"Major Cochran. John Cochran."

Gerard knew that muffled voice. It was General Soutine's large servant. But what was he doing here? Recognizing his father's name made him stagger to his feet and stumble toward the road below. There was a carriage parked there, perhaps two carriages. He squeezed his eyes shut and steadied himself on an upended cannon.

"There he is," said someone by the carriage. He said it in French. The voice sounded like General Soutine's. But why? He squeezed his eyelids shut and felt himself swaying. Suddenly someone large picked him up and carried him.

"Father?"

"We cannot find your father," Condé said in French with his nasal accent.

How odd that the words translated themselves in his head without the slightest delay even though his head ached horribly. But his mother had always spoken French to him. She said someday it would be important for him to know it.

"I must find my father."

"Quickly, into the carriage," Soutine ordered.

"I must find my father," Gerard repeated in French.

"We will try, but you are hurt and must get attention soon."

He found himself laid on the seat opposite the general and struggled to sit up while Condé wound a bandage around his head. Gerard felt himself spiraling down into the blankness of sleep, but he could still hear. Condé exited, jostling the well-sprung vehicle.

The carriage lunched forward with Condé calling for Major Cochran from his vantage point at the back. Good, they were going to search. But why? Why had General Soutine come all the way from Paris to look for an officer in the British army? No matter how grateful Gerard was for the aid, he could not forget this man was his grandfather's enemy. But his brain was too racked with pain to be able to attribute anything sinister to the man's motives.

He felt the old man's concern as he drew a blanket over Gerard. That was enough. Then all the faces he was picturing in his mind, his father, Tully, Soutine, Condé, and Crispin blurred into one that was gone in a swirl of fog where one name was still shouted in vain.

****

Paris, June 22, 1815

Lights danced behind his eyelids, forming strange patterns of red and black. What was he seeing? Blood and smoke? Gerard let his eyes flicker open, then clenched them shut against a blaze of sunshine that seemed to burn a hole through his vision. He could see the hole on the inside of his eyelids, lit along the edges with green fire. Then it grew smaller and eventually dissipated to a reddish glow.

His head ached a bit less, but his body felt as though it had been racked. He experimented with moving his arms and legs. They functioned more or less but had no strength. Then he remembered that some French cavalry had ridden over him. Small wonder that he ached in every limb.

A tray rattled and he squinted at the source. Condé with his great gentle hands pouring something into a mug. Tea would be wonderful. He struggled to get an arm under him and rise. But Condé slid him up against a bank of pillows as though he were a rag doll.

"Can you hold this?" he asked in French.

"*Oui.*" Gerard took the warm cup and cradled it to his lips. It was broth, not tea, but it was fragrant and hot. It reminded him how thirsty he was. He asked for water in French. Then he remembered his father and was almost afraid to ask the question. "Did you find him?"

Condé gave him an assessing look, then shook his

head.

Gerard held his breath for a minute before he asked. "Is he dead?"

Condé shrugged and put the tray across his lap.

He tried to eat but nothing seemed to have a taste now. Finally he lay back and let his mind empty of everything.

****

When next he awoke, General Soutine was watching him.

Gerard was afraid to ask about his father. Instead he asked the second question on his mind. "Why did you help me?"

"Did you imagine I would let anyone I know perish on that battlefield?"

"But why were you there looking for Father?"

"Your father owes me a debt."

"I can pay you if I still have his money."

"Your life is payment enough."

"My life? But *you* saved me."

"I did not mean you had to die to repay this debt of honor but to live."

Gerard stared at him, thinking he resembled someone he knew. "I do not understand."

"Because of your father, my child died. I want you to live in return."

"But my father will want me back. Besides, he would never harm a child."

Soutine looked away toward the window. "We do not know where he is. I promise you, if your father lives, we will find him."

Nothing could have hurt Gerard more. This meant they did not think his father had survived. "I must go to the battlefield and search. There will be soldiers there who will know him." Gerard managed to stand up. Then there was a roaring in his ears and he pitched back onto the bed.

"The battlefield is far away in Belgium. You cannot possibly go there."

"Far away? Where are we?"

"Paris, of course. That is where I live most of the time."

Enemy territory but only if the English had lost. Gerard had the strength for only one more question. "Who won?"

"Wellington and Blucher. But it was in doubt until the very end."

Gerard sighed. That meant there would be English soldiers in Paris again and he could talk to them.

****

He was alone when he next woke up. When he could stand, he carefully searched the room. He found his father's store of coins in the bureau, still in the money belt. He had well over a hundred pounds to aid him in his search. Soutine was no thief. Neither was Condé. So he did just want Gerard to stay here. But why? How could an English soldier's brat make up for the loss of a French child? He also opened the small packet of documents in the money belt. Perhaps that's why his father had given him the belt, so he would have his identification papers.

When he read his baptismal certificate he was stunned. He was nearly nineteen, a full year older than he'd been told. His father had lied about that to keep him from enlisting. In spite of this betrayal he felt himself smiling at the ruthlessness of the subterfuge.

There was also one letter and the contents almost

choked him. It was from General Cochran and prohibited his son from ever returning to Old Stand. Finally he understood the scope of his father's pain.

That night he was able to dine at table with Soutine, passing the critical muster on the forms of a multi-course meal. They ended with coffee and a dessert. Since they dined late, it was near dark by the time Condé appeared with the coffee tray. He was a strange servant, saying little and almost communicating more through body language than speech. He was tense tonight, and Gerard did not think it was because he was presenting a new sort of trifle.

When everything had been cleared away, Soutine poured Gerard two fingers of brandy. Gerard stared at the ruby liquid as though it were blood coating the inside of the glass. He looked across at Soutine and read the regret in the man's eyes. He knew what he was going to tell him and, though he did not want to hear it, he felt some sympathy for the old man. Enough to prevent Gerard chiding him for something that was none of his doing.

He took up the glass and downed half in one swallow. "He's dead, then, isn't he?"

Soutine stared at him with pain in his eyes. Carefully he unfolded an English newspaper, the *Times*, and laid it before Gerard. His finger ran down one column to arrive like the skeletal digit of the grim reaper at his father's name. The notice was brief and only one of many still being listed two weeks after the battle. Missing and presumed dead. So Soutine had still been looking for his father in a way.

A weight pressed on Gerard and he felt unable to move from the chair. His purpose had been lost. The only goal in his life was to return to his father, and that had been snatched away. His beloved father must have been robbed and stripped of any identification, then thrown into a common grave. The search was over before it had begun. What was he to do with himself now? It hardly mattered. He tried to stand and staggered. He remembered Condé helping him to bed, but nothing more that night.

****

The next morning was worse because he was sober and remembered his father's death again. It was like losing him twice, and he wondered how many mornings he would awake to the realization like a fresh wound to the heart. He went over in his mind the day of the battle and wondered if he should have disobeyed orders earlier. Could he have made a difference? One thing a soldier should never do is look back.

But he was not a soldier. His name would never appear on the list of missing, and he would drop from the sight of the military world. He wondered what had become of Tully but he had no energy to find him. His father's batman would go back to England with all the others. Gerard did not have to write his grandfather at all. The old man had probably seen or heard about the notice in the *Times*, of course, and that was as much as he deserved.

Gerard had no future to look forward to. For several days he moved like a dead person, replying to Soutine or Condé if he heard them, but often not hearing them, just staring out the window of the old hotel into the summer rains.

"I said, it is time you went to school," Soutine almost shouted across the breakfast table.

Gerard looked up at him over the toast he had been

crumbling onto his plate. "My father gave me the name of an instructor in England. I had almost forgotten. That is what I was supposed to do with the money, go to England and find the school."

"Nonsense. There are many excellent schools right here in Paris, better than any English school."

Gerard did not argue with him and followed Condé when he led him to the Académie de Paris that day. Soutine went as well but in a sedan chair. There was a lengthy interview with the director, a course of study chosen, which at Gerard's insistence included medicine, then some inquiry as to Gerard's skill in French. A few minutes of speech convinced the man he could hold his own. They left Gerard there and he developed a mild interest in the classes that met that day. He also encountered several young Frenchmen who might be a problem.

"*Anglais*, you want to learn how to be a Frenchman?" one of them asked in heavily accented English.

"I already know that. I want to learn how to be a better Frenchman," he said in French. Too late, as they held him against a wall and pummeled him, he realized he had said, "…better than a Frenchman." Perhaps his language skills left something to be desired after all. He vowed to stay out of fights in future. Though his father had always been tolerant of brawling, Gerard sensed that split lips and bruised ribs would disturb the general more.

Besides, he felt different, as though there was no fight left in him. Yes, the English had won, but Gerard personally felt defeated and like a prisoner of war, the only English prisoner still held by the French. And he no longer had the will to get away.

When he left the building, Condé was waiting for him. It did occur to Gerard that the building had more than one door and gate, but Condé had trusted him and he saw no reason to violate that.

That night Soutine asked about his classmates at the dinner table and Gerard shrugged. "I have not much in common with them."

"Even less if you plan to pursue medicine as a career, but you will soon grow tired of that. Two things are missing. You need to learn some proper horsemanship and fencing. Saturday you will ride in a park where I know the horse master who teaches dressage, and in the afternoon have fencing lessons at the Salon du Burgh. I know the fencing master personally."

Gerard realized he could not keep a gleam of interest out of his face. He'd learned how to ride as a child, but dressage was much more demanding, and fencing was an art that had always intrigued him.

"Does that please you?"

"Very much. I like horses."

"And tonight we go to a play by Racine. You will like that as well. Next week we attend the ballet. But first you need better clothes, evening wear. My tailor will be here early tomorrow to measure you."

Gerard opened his mouth but did not object. He had been wearing clothes Condé must have bought in a street stall, and he had been expecting to live in seclusion with Soutine, playing chess with him to amuse him or reading to him, which helped with his own grammar and accent. He had not expected a life of his own, so he finally said, "I thank you for all your care of me and all you have spent already. But what will people think of you if they find out you are supporting an Englishman, and one with no claim on you?"

"They have no right to speculate on why you live with me or how that came to be. You have my leave to tell them it is none of their business."

"You are right. It matters not what anyone in Paris thinks of me." Was this what it would always be like, thanking your jailer? He shrugged off the notion. He could walk out of Soutine's life if he wished, but he owed the man something and he wasn't even sure what it was. That debt of honor. How could he make up for the loss of a child? There was something else, some puzzle he had not worked out yet, that made him reluctant to leave. Besides, he had no place he wanted to go.

He remembered an estate where he had stayed with his mother for a short while when he was very young. It had a huge house, a hedge maze, and sheep. But where it was or who it belonged to he had no idea. When English troops bivouacked, the officers rated the best lodgings available though often that was a hovel. The estate had not seemed like campaign lodgings because his father had been missing.

Chapter Three

Paris, August, 1815

He had come alone to the theater tonight since Soutine's leg was bothering him. Alone except for Condé dozing in the back of the box. Gerard had become accustomed to life with Soutine and drifted with the flow of school, chess playing, the theater, and other social engagements. His clothes marked him now as a prosperous though perhaps foppish young gentleman, and since he perceived Soutine was training him to act that part, he applied himself. Gerard suspected he was destined to embarrass his English relatives someday. If that was Soutine's purpose, he was not ready to reveal it. But why would he expect Gerard to cooperate? He was tired of being a pawn, but there was no purpose to his life that Gerard could see. Besides, it gratified him to amuse the old man. It was very much like being on stage.

This was a new play by a little-known playwright, and he was making notes with a small pencil of all the good lines so he could relate them to Soutine when they got home. He would be waiting up and would ask. There were many amusing jokes, which Gerard recorded faithfully, picturing the general chuckling in his rich deep voice when Gerard recited them.

As the first act drew to a close, he noticed a man in the box across the way staring at him in a most insistent manner. Gerard tried to ignore his speaking looks, but the other occupant of the box was a lovely girl with long golden hair, and her gaze was full of concern. What could she possibly be worried about? There was something about them, the cut of their clothes. Suddenly it hit Gerard that they were English. Perhaps he was a soldier in civilian dress and the girl his wife come to join him. Yet they looked so alike Gerard rather suspected they were sister and brother. He decided to speak to him. There was always a chance the man had known his father or knew more about his death. He had met at least half a dozen English officers since the Waterloo campaign but none he knew well, and after a while he'd decided to stop asking about his father. He was dead, that much was certain. Where he lay, no one knew, but that could be said of hundreds of men.

Gerard knew better than to announce to the dozing Condé that he was going to speak to an Englishman. When the audience stood for the intermission, he turned to his guard-companion and asked if he wanted him to get wine for them. Condé nodded and settled himself more firmly in the corner, not at all shy about letting his charge run this errand. Gerard could see the other man leaving his box as well and stayed long enough to watch which way he went. Then he made his way through the crowd to intercept him. When he feared he had lost the fellow, someone grabbed him by the shoulder and said, "Gerard? Gerard Cochran?"

Gerard turned to face him. "How do you know me? Are you with the army?"

"No, I am Charles Chandler. Major Cochran was my cousin—well, second cousin."

Gerard could not help smiling. "He spoke of you."

In the busy bustle of the hallway with French jibes and laughter flying around them, Gerard felt his English lying heavy on his tongue as though it was the foreign language.

"Then you *are* Gerard Cochran. What are you doing in Paris? When we got no word about you in Brussels and Ostend, we assumed you were dead. I spent a deal of time asking after you."

"I was rescued by a friend, a friend of my father's. I live with him now."

"I have been talking to every officer I have run across, and no one knew what had happened to you. Your father would want you to come back to England."

"England? But why?"

"How can you ask that? England is your home, or should be."

"I was born there but have never lived there."

"Your grandfather wants you to come."

Gerard recalled the bitter letter. "Forgive me if I find that hard to believe. We cannot talk here. The intermission will soon be over and I still have to purchase wine. Can we meet somewhere?"

"I will be in Paris another three weeks on business. Name a place."

"I attend the Académie de Paris. Can you be there at noon tomorrow?"

"Yes, I will manage it."

He turned to go, then spun again. "Chandler. The lady in the box? Your wife?"

He smiled. "No, my sister. I'll bring her with me tomorrow. You may meet her then."

Gerard was late getting back to the box, but all Condé cared about was the wine. He did not notice

Gerard's guarded glances toward the beauty in the box across the way. Though she did her share of looking, her gaze was sympathetic rather than admiring or sexually alluring. In that respect she was nothing like the women he had met in Spain or in France. They had all wanted something from him. And this girl seemed different, as though she could care about him for his own sake. Of course she was very young. That was probably why she looked so sweet. Finally Gerard decided he must turn his attention back to the stage if he was to give an accounting of the play to the general.

****

Soutine was waiting up when they got home. While Condé made coffee, Gerard read all the lines he had recorded. Soutine laughed at all the humorous bits over coffee, cheese, and fruit before he asked, "What is wrong, Gerard? You look worried."

If ever there was a time to tell him, it was now. He owed him too much to deceive him even though he had no qualms about hiding things from Condé. "There was an Englishman at the theater tonight." Gerard took a long drink of the hot brew laced with milk. He was used to coffee now rather than tea.

The general leaned back in the great padded chair. "Did he speak to you?"

"Yes, he is Father's cousin, Charles Chandler, here on business." Gerard chose an apple and bit into it.

"Did he ask you to return to England with him?"

"Yes." Gerard stared at Soutine, trying to judge his reaction to this news, but the old man remained as inscrutable as ever, his heavy eyelids half-closed over his glittering eyes just as he looked when they were playing chess.

Soutine's right hand gripped his cane. "And what did you say?"

"That I was fixed here. I see no point in going."

Condé handed Soutine a medicine glass. The old man looked at it with disfavor, drained it, then shuddered. "Did your father ever tell you why he did not return to his family estate?"

Gerard thought of the letter but did not want to confess that horrid banishment to Soutine. "Yes, my grandfather was a bit of a tyrant."

Soutine clenched his teeth, then sighed. "It was more than that. His father, General Cochran, disowned him for marrying a Frenchwoman."

"So he condemned Mother, never having met her?"

"And condemned her and you to follow the drum. Your father was too proud to allow her to stay with her French relatives, more's the pity. She might still be alive if that were the case."

Gerard stared at him, expecting the names of the relatives, but Soutine's face was so sad he had not the heart to probe him. "Father said you were an enemy of Grandfather's, which immediately made me think you could not be such a bad fellow."

The general laughed. "So you have developed a disdain for your grandfather without ever having met him."

"I suppose. But that was his doing. It confirms my decision never to go there."

"Hmm." Soutine groaned, the sound like the rumbling of an old bear. "This cousin may not give up so easily. He will try to get you back." Soutine looked up at him with that sad smile.

"I doubt that he is sincere. If my grandfather disliked

my father so much, I'm sure he will not like me either."

"Not liking you may not be the issue. He may still want to control you."

"But why?" Gerard put down his cup. This was the most he had learned about his family in his whole life.

"Your father's older brother died. John was the second son. By English law, now you are the heir."

"I don't care," Gerard flung out as he stood and walked to the window. "If that's why I matter to him now, how can he reasonably expect any loyalty from me?"

"Alfred Cochran is not a reasonable man, not when I knew him."

Gerard stared at him. "What was the great fight between you two? Most French and English officers find themselves in accord when not shooting at each other."

"He stole something from me."

"Stole?"

"A woman. I do not look like it now, but I was quite a romantic fellow at one time."

"He stole your woman?" Gerard winked at Condé who clamped a huge paw over his mouth to suppress a snort of laughter.

"Don't joke, Gerard. It was not like that. She was a lady and he wooed her with false words. I was the one who loved her. What are you thinking?"

Gerard threw his hands up. "That the lady should have had the choice. Only property is stolen, not people."

The general laughed. "If only you knew. Now go to bed before I have Condé beat you."

"Very well, I see I have dug far too deep into the truth to suit you, sir."

"Young rascal."

****

The next morning Juliet was grimacing over some ill-made tea in their hotel suite when Charles entered and poured himself a brandy. She frowned at him drinking this early but when she tasted the tea again admitted there was some excuse. She was wearing a new dress she'd had made and was not at all sure she liked the tiny capped sleeves and low bodice in spite of what her maid Sophie said.

"What did you think of Gerard?" He came and sat with her.

"I never got to meet him. He seemed to scowl a lot. And he looks to be a bit of a dandy, but I'm no judge." She put down her cup and saucer with finality.

"Not when I talked to him. I think he simply needs guidance. I am to meet him today at noon. I promised you would come."

"And my purpose is to lure him into Uncle's clutches?"

"More like your clutches. One reason for convincing him to come to England is to get you your freedom early. Just think. If you marry him, your affairs will be turned over to your husband and you can live anywhere. And even after I marry Melanthe I still won't come into my money for four years."

"I had not thought of that before, but what if he turns out to be worse than Claude?"

Charles gave a snort of laughter. "Juliet, come now. Who could be worse than Claude?"

"You are right, I'm sure. I wanted to come when I felt so sorry for Gerard and his father. Now I am losing my courage. By all we have heard, John really is dead. We should bring his son home." She got up and walked to the window. "How can Paris still be so beautiful after all the years of war? Appearances mean nothing."

"You'd better come and find out if you can stomach the fellow. He seems biddable to me. And you must marry someone."

"Why? Why must I marry anyone?" She turned to Charles and he tilted his head to one side, meaning he was considering what she said.

"In point of fact, you don't have to marry. Father left us his fortune in equal shares. But neither of us has access to anything except what the general gives us."

"Until we are twenty-five."

"And that's seven years away for you. If you can't like the fellow, then we just forget that part of it, but I really think we should try to bring him home for his own sake."

Juliet shook her head. "Poor boy. It must be horrible losing your father to war."

Charles frowned. "I don't think it matters how you lose them."

"I'm so sorry to remind you." She went to him and hugged him. "Charles, what would our lives be like if Father had not gone down in that ship, if Mother had not died of despair?"

"I imagine we'd be living in our house in London. You might be married by now."

"And you?"

"I would still be chasing wool contracts. I would not even know Melanthe."

"And you do love her?" She released him to scan his face.

He pursed his lips and frowned. "Perhaps I just feel sorry for her. But my instinct to protect her cannot spring from a bad part of my character. I think by now she is in love with me. So it would be ill-done of me to ignore her expectations since she has none other. Besides, I don't love anyone else, and the general does like to keep the wealth in the family."

"Then we must make a push to get to know Gerard. If I don't want him, perhaps Melanthe will take a fancy to him and you can let him cut you out with her."

Charles laughed. "Quite the little matchmaker. But I warn you, people do not always go on as you think they will."

****

When Gerard slipped out the side entrance of the school, Charles was waiting, and his beautiful sister was with him. She had worn her hair long at the theater, glorious locks of it coiling around each side of her delicate neck. Now it was tucked under a straw bonnet except for some stray wisps that danced in the gentle morning breeze. Her jonquil gown made her look vulnerable, like someone needing protection.

"Allow me to present my sister, Juliet Chandler. This is your cousin, Gerard Cochran."

"*Mon plaisir*—I mean, my pleasure, Miss Chandler. I am so used to French now that I have to think about English." He looked into her blue eyes and realized here was a woman who could never deceive or betray a man. She was innocence itself. He also realized that, after taking her hand and making a pretense of kissing it, he should have released it and finally he did, then bowed awkwardly.

"I wish my French were that good," she said as she rose from a curtsey. Her voice was intimate and husky, as though she was under some strong emotion. But what?

"Where shall we go?" Charles asked.

Gerard looked over his shoulder. "I know a café. We will dine. I usually don't bother with a midday meal, but we cannot talk in the street." He took Juliet's arm on the pretext of guiding her safely across the thoroughfare and simply neglected to release her until he had seated them at a sidewalk table and received permission to order for them. Gerard requested a soup he knew was good, with bread and cheese and a good wine.

Chandler turned to him. "That servant I saw you with, he isn't just a footman, is he?"

"Condé?" Gerard shrugged. "I used to think he was my jailer, but I could easily evade him now if I wished. He goes out with me only at night now." He tasted the wine presented, shrugged, and the waiter poured.

"Where are you living?" Charles asked.

Gerard felt some embarrassment to admit he was staying with his grandfather's enemy—and his father's, if he mistook not. "Why do you wish to know?"

"You are heir to your grandfather's estate now that your father is dead."

Gerard shrugged and noticed Juliet looking at him with concern. "Yes, I know it, but surely there is another to fill that role."

"Not now that we know you are alive," Juliet said. "If you return with us, both Nash and Claude will be displaced."

Gerard smiled and took a sip of wine. "Then don't tell them I am alive."

"But I have written home already," Charles said. "The general will want you to come."

Gerard pushed his glass in small circles on the old wooden table. He had made his decision, chosen to stay with Soutine, and now they were showing him a different way. "I wager he will not. If he has such a disdain for things French, he will not want me."

Charles leaned across the table. "That accent would disappear after a month or two in Northamptonshire."

He laughed. "But I don't want it to. I have worked a long time to speak French like a Parisian."

"You mean to stay here?" Juliet asked in disbelief.

Gerard shrugged. "Why not?"

The waiter brought their food then, and Gerard could see Juliet and Charles trade dubious looks until the man left them.

"What will you do?" Charles asked as he picked up his spoon and looked at the bowl suspiciously.

Gerard grinned. "It's leek soup, not a bowl of poison, Chandler."

That made Juliet giggle. She had already sampled the soup. A woman of courage in spite of her delicate looks.

"What will you do?" Chandler repeated.

"I have not decided yet. I have some thought to study medicine, and Paris is a far better place for that than London."

Juliet cleared her throat. "When I mentioned displacing Nash and his son, I meant that would be a good thing. Your Uncle Nash has a viperish tongue and Claude's always been a bully. I can't count the number of times I have had to rescue our young cousin Jack from him. If he ever inherited the title he would be impossible."

"But if you are only cousins, surely you don't have to put up with them. You can live somewhere else. But forgive me if I presume too much. Perhaps you are not free to do as you wish."

Charles sighed. "If Uncle were to die in the next four years, we would both be under Nash's thumb, and he might try to force Juliet to wed Claude, whom she detests."

Gerard felt his head snap toward her. She was so beautiful, and now her cheeks flamed with color. Any woman would be embarrassed to have someone think her a helpless possession. "But he can't really force you, can he?" He stared at the girl and her intensity impressed him. She didn't seem vulnerable when she held her head up and looked back at him. He'd wager no one could compel Juliet to do anything, but at what cost to her he hated to think.

"He can make our lives miserable," Charles said. "But if you come, Great-Uncle would be distracted from both of them. Your father was the middle brother, older than Nash by a year or two, so eventually you would become the owner of the estate and half-interest in one of the most prosperous wool mills in the north. Uncle and Father were partners in the mill."

"Is that supposed to lure me to England? It wasn't enough to hold Father."

"The rift between your father and your grandfather was none of your doing. I tell you, Uncle wants you home." Charles reached for the cheese and gnawed a piece of the hard French bread as an alternative to the soup.

"We each make our own path and choose our own punishment for our mistakes."

Chandler looked surprised. "No one wants to punish you. You are too young to realize your loyalty should lie with your family in England."

"I wasn't speaking of me. My grandfather set his

course and has reaped loneliness. Let him live with that."

"What do you know of retribution?" Juliet asked, her fine brows drawn together.

He stared at her in fascination. He could read her face like a book. "I have been present on some of the most grisly battlefields of the last decade. I suspect I know far more of it than you."

She glanced down, her lips trembling until she set them in a thin determined line. That made him feel small to taunt her with that comment. He knew nothing about Juliet. She might be far more courageous than he had ever been.

"Forgive me. You have come here to invite me home and I am being churlish. All I want is some news, not to make you both uncomfortable. I know little about my family, and I confess I am curious."

Charles cleared his throat. "Besides your Uncle Nash and his son Claude, Nash's mother Helen is yet living. The general's younger sister Emma, a widow, lives there as well, with her two children."

Juliet clasped her hands in her lap. "Our mother Edith was a niece to General Cochran, the only child of his brother, who is dead. Our parents are both deceased."

"Not a prolific family," Gerard said.

Charles nodded. "Hence the search for the heir."

Juliet looked him in the eye. "I have thought about what your life must have been like and feel sad for you. There is no reason you should help us. You owe us nothing."

"Indeed, I would do anything I could to help you. But here in Paris there is an old man to whom I owe a great deal—my life, in fact. I do not feel I can abandon him to follow a whim."

"Could he not come with you?" she suggested, leaning forward over the table in her eagerness.

"To England?" Gerard shook his head as he discarded the thought.

"Why not? I would think he would be glad to see you safely bestowed."

"Yes, a wonderful idea," Chandler agreed. "We'll invite him to go with us, and he can judge for himself if it is not better for you to take your rightful place than to stay here."

"What is his name?" Juliet prompted. She perched on the edge of the wobbly wooden chair, the meal forgotten.

"He can barely walk now, but I assure you that if my benefactor ever met my grandfather there would be blood on the table within the hour." He took a sip of wine, keeping them in suspense. He must be honest with them. Once they knew the truth they would let him alone. And yet he wanted to prolong the moment when they wanted him to come with them. He did not want to let go of the possibility of being with Juliet even though he knew nothing could come of it. Was he falling in love with her in less than an hour?

"But who is he?" she insisted.

"General Henri Soutine."

Charles gaped at him.

"Retired of course," Gerard added, then drained his wineglass.

"A Frenchman?" Juliet asked.

"General Cochran's mortal enemy," Charles supplied. "Whatever we do, we must never tell Great-Uncle where you have been living."

"I see," Juliet said. "Will you at least wait until we

receive an answer to Charles' letter?" She reached for Gerard's hand and held it. At that moment, with her small competent hand grasping his in her effort to help him, if she had asked him to move the earth he would have made an effort.

"Yes, of course, but I don't think it will change anything. It has been a pleasure meeting you." He drew her hand to his lips and kissed it for real, then reluctantly released her. "Now I must get back to class."

He went to settle the account with the waiter, but when he came back outside they were waiting for him, so he took Juliet's arm again and escorted her toward the Académie with Charles walking on her other side. He began to wonder if even Juliet, sweet and innocent though she was, had an instinct for using that to convince him to come with them. They were silent for the walk back.

"How can I get word to you?" Charles asked.

Gerard pulled a stub of pencil from his pocket and scratched his direction on the back of one of Chandler's cards. "You can send a note here."

"Will you receive it?"

"Yes, of course. I told the general about you and he was not at all surprised. I am not really a prisoner, you know."

He looked back as he crossed the street and realized that Juliet did not believe him, that he would chose to stay with an old enemy rather than return to the bosom of his family however neglectful they had been. How sweet of her but how naïve. Besides, he had not yet puzzled out why Soutine had rescued him, and he could not leave that question unanswered.

As Gerard turned back toward the door, Juliet

watched him with concern. Yes, he wore foppish clothes and lace cuffs, yet he moved and spoke with the assurance of a grown man. He had been trampled by life and resented that. She could relate since she felt trampled as well. He was perhaps too sure he was right, but then, he had lost both his mother and his father. That had made her grow up fast. If he had not been willing to make decisions, he might be dead now.

She worried for him yet felt he would be able to survive since he had already come through so much. But she so wanted to get to know him, to take him home with them where he could reach his full potential. Or would he become like Nash and Claude, waiting for handouts? Even she and Charles had to depend on their great-uncle but not by choice. Sometimes it seemed like the others were just waiting for the general to die.

"What are you thinking?" Charles asked as they walked arm in arm toward their hotel.

"About whether Gerard might be right."

"What do you mean?" Charles guided her across a thoroughfare, though she was the one who dragged back on his arm so they did not get trampled by a carriage team.

"I want him to come with us to take his rightful place, but I don't want to see him under Great-Uncle's thumb."

"He's too young to be on his own."

"He can't be more than a few years younger than you, and he's seen so much more, been through so much more."

"That's hardly my fault."

"It's not a flaw, Charles, but a condition of life. I wish he had not suffered so much, yet that might be the making of him."

"What are you saying, that we should let him stay here? Great-Uncle is counting on us. We cannot fail him."

She shook her head. "I don't know what I'm saying. I simply feel we have created a turning point in Gerard's life and we have to respect whatever decision he makes."

"He's hardly competent to decide if he should whistle a fortune down the wind. He could come with us and then return if he doesn't like Great-Uncle."

"And Soutine's health?"

"What I suspect is that Soutine is using that to hold Gerard for whatever evil purpose he has in mind, and that our cousin is not as free to come and go as he thinks he is."

"What could Soutine be planning? He saved Gerard's life."

"He's turning him into a dandy. You said it yourself. Gerard needs to go to his family before he becomes Soutine's puppet."

"I hardly think that is likely. Gerard is self-assured. No one will control him if he does not wish it."

"Do you want to know what I think?" he asked.

She smiled. "I feel you are going to tell me anyway."

"I think Soutine is going to use Gerard to embarrass General Cochran, turn him into some sort of society fop and then present him in London as the heir to Old Stand. If Soutine controls Gerard, he can ruin Old Stand."

"That seems very unlikely. You've never even met General Soutine. How can you make such assumptions about him?"

"What other explanation can there be for him capturing the grandson of an old enemy? He wants his revenge."

"Capturing? Until we find out, you should not let your imagination run wild."

"Juliet, I mean to bring Gerard home with or without your help. If I went to the army, they would deport him. I'm just trying to get him to come voluntarily."

"I will do my best to help you, but you are always warning me to take into account that other people have minds of their own. Let me assure you that applies to Gerard as well."

"How could you know him so well after only a few minutes' conversation?"

"I'm not sure, but I do understand him in part because we are so much alike."

Charles frowned at her in puzzlement, but she thought he must already be scheming a way to get Gerard out of France.

****

Paris, September 1815

Gerard awoke to another day of suspense. He both wanted and didn't want his grandfather to want him. But when he thought about wanting to be wanted, the image of a grizzled old man was replaced by Juliet's smiling countenance. Was it possible she could want him even if his grandfather did not? And if that was the case, what could he do about it? He had no expectations or fortune. Not much more than a hundred gold guineas stashed in his drawer and those bequeathed by his father. Lately he had been wearing the money belt as some sort of talisman, a connection to his father though it gave him no advice on what to do.

And what if the old tartar said to come? Of course his answer should be the same no matter what. He should not go with Charles and Juliet simply because he was attracted to her. The vague future that he imagined or avoided thinking about, by turns, now pressed on him as a necessity. If he was not to go to England, then he must plan what he meant to do. He was at a fork in the road and he must decide what lay down each path.

He would ask Soutine if he could study medicine in earnest. If he could do that, he would stay in Paris with goodwill. He would never be wealthy, but he might be useful if for no other purpose than to ease the old man's pain.

When he came downstairs, a note from Charles lay by his breakfast plate. It had not been opened. Soutine did not inquire about it. In fact, he managed not to look at it, quite a trick through the whole meal. Gerard desperately wanted to know what it said but decided to open it on the way to the Académie. When he finally tore it open, he found Chandler requested to meet at noon at the same restaurant but did not say why. More suspense.

Gerard barely attended the morning lectures. If the beautiful Juliet accompanied her brother, he would at least get to see her one more time even if his grandfather did not want him. Finally he walked out the back door of the school and met them at the café. They had already ordered a meal and the waiter was bringing it as he sat down. Juliet was wearing blue today and the color complemented her golden looks. Her beautiful hair was long and loose under a chip straw hat, and the fringe on her shawl drifted in the breeze, adding languor to her smiling invitation.

"He wants you to come to England," Chandler said abruptly.

Gerard could see Juliet send her brother a speaking

look and wondered if this was the truth. "May I see the letter?"

"You don't believe me?" Chandler seemed affronted and not at all forthcoming with the document.

"Then let me show you a letter. It was in my father's money belt." Gerard had been prepared for this and had placed the offending document in his pocket. He handed Chandler the much-creased piece of parchment.

He opened it carefully, read, and shook his head. "This must have been written in a great fit of anger."

"May I?" Juliet asked and Gerard nodded.

Chandler shrugged and handed it to her. "My great-uncle wrote that almost twenty years ago and it was to a son who had done his utmost to disobey him."

"You can't cut off a branch without losing the fruit as well. He should have thought of that."

Gerard saw tears in Juliet's eyes as she slowly folded the letter and handed it back to him. "I'm sure he thinks of it every time he looks at Claude, who is not a promising fruit on the family tree," she said in a tremulous voice.

Gerard was sorry she had sampled that venom, but she had asked. "I am not surprised he has lived to regret his mistake. Your letter?" Gerard held his hand out, palm up.

Chandler reluctantly handed him a page. The writing was so spidery as to be almost indecipherable. He had to read through a lot of business instructions before he came to the bit about him, almost an afterthought.

"I am constrained to settle matters as regards my heir. If there is a chance the boy is Gerard, you must bring him back at all costs and immediately. We can't have him loose in France." Gerard chuckled. "*Très drôle.* He doesn't really believe I am Gerard."

"But you look so much like your father and even like the general. You will convince him," Juliet insisted.

"I don't want to convince him. I don't care what he thinks."

"But you cannot turn your back on a fortune, even if you don't want the connection," Chandler insisted.

"Yes, I can. Are we going to eat?"

As Gerard and Juliet both made a pretense of consuming the roast fowl, Chandler used every argument he could think of to convince Gerard to visit his grandfather. He even promised to bring him back to France if he did not like England.

Juliet's arguments were more persuasive because he indeed wanted to be with her. But he saw small chance of ever getting to wed her even if he did insinuate himself into the family. She was too fine, too innocent to be interested in a war orphan.

"I am going to be late," he said as he rose to return to school.

"May we write to you?" Chandler insisted. "I don't want to lose track of you."

Gerard saw the pain in Juliet's eyes and regretted it. "It would be best if you did forget me. It has been a pleasure, Juliet. Keep working on that accent."

"Wait," Juliet called and stood as if she would go after him.

He came back and took her hands. "What is it? You seem in so much pain over this and you hardly know me."

"My distress is selfish. If you do not come forward as a candidate for my hand, I will be forced to marry

Claude."

"What?" Gerard staggered and nearly upset a chair.

"You owe us nothing," Chandler said, "but if you should ever reconsider, please come to Old Stand. I can give you the direction."

"I know it well enough. My father wrote it down for me."

"So you see," Chandler reasoned, "if he wanted you to forever shun the place, he would never have told you where it was. Is there no chance you might make peace with your grandfather even though your father never could?"

"My father would be alive if he had not been cast out."

"Would he?" Juliet asked with tears illuminating the brilliance of her blue eyes.

"What are you saying?" He realized he had been clutching her hands and let go of them.

"Would he indeed be alive?" she insisted. "They fought over his desire to join the army."

Charles stood and looked at Gerard. "I corresponded with your father. I was to meet with him in March, but we left it too late."

"Are you saying it was my father's wish for me to return?"

"Think, Gerard," Juliet pleaded. "Even if your father had come to England and reconciled, would he have stayed out of that battle? Or would he have donned his uniform again to fight the old foe?"

He stared at her as though she were a gypsy telling him his fortune and he was listening to the truth. How could she know his father so well? "You have given me much to think about," he mumbled.

"We must leave for England in a few days," Charles said. "Here is the direction of our hotel. Please come with us just for a visit. You can return if you dislike it."

"I thank you again for your concern, but do not look for me." Gerard kissed Juliet's hand one last time, then turned and left them. It would be easy to go with them, to let himself be enchanted by Juliet's beauty and Chandler's friendship. He felt himself to be at a crossroads. He could choose obligation to Soutine and duty, though his notion to become a doctor was self-imposed. Or he could follow the path of the English landed gentry. Perhaps an easier life. But what should make Juliet admire him, if she did admire him, was the path that would carry him away from her. Somehow he could not appreciate the irony of it.

Chapter Four

That might have ended it, had not Soutine decided to attend the theater himself the next night. Now, why would he take that notion into his head when he knew the English cousins were still in Paris? Gerard had half expected Chandler to approach Soutine, who stared at Charles and Juliet with an odd light in his eyes. Gerard could never read him. Was he looking victorious? Though Juliet sent them sympathetic looks, Chandler merely glared at them throughout the performance. Gerard almost toyed with the notion of introducing them during the intermission, but Soutine had no plans to leave the box and Chandler did not come to them.

When they returned to the house, Soutine called Gerard to his chamber on the ground floor. "That fellow in the box across the theater, was that him, your cousin?"

Gerard sat on the windowsill. "Yes. I won't go with him, hence the looks of disapproval."

"Oh, I think those were directed against me."

"No matter."

"So you have decided to take up the task of punishing your grandfather where your father left off?"

Gerard could scarcely believe his ears. "It was my father who was wronged."

"Perhaps. Many people are wronged in life. It is seldom clear cut or one-sided. Come to think of it, that is how wars start."

"Did you really know my father well enough to know this?"

"I did not know what was in his heart. I do not know what is in yours, for that matter, but I do not think it harbors revenge."

"What are you saying, that you want me to go?"

Soutine looked at him with his eyes wide open, not the shuttered look that was his trademark. Gerard thought he should be able to read the man's soul, but there was only regret writ on his old face.

"No," he said finally, closing his eyes. "I do not want you to leave."

"Then I will not," he said and walked toward the door.

"But I think you should go."

Gerard halted and turned to regard Soutine in profile this time. He was more inscrutable than ever. "What do you mean? Go and return?"

"If you wish."

"And what of Juliet? They have some notion I can save her from a bad marriage if I am the heir."

The old man tilted his head to look at him. "Do you love her?"

"I think I could love her if I let myself love anyone."

Soutine's voice cracked on a laugh. "You talk in riddles, Gerard. We will discuss it further in the morning."

****

Try as he might, Gerard could not get to sleep. What could they possibly discuss about this in the morning? Soutine was old and injured, like a wounded bear. With only Condé to take care of him, he might not survive until Gerard had visited his family and returned. But the temptation was there to actually see England and to confront the old villain who had cast his father out.

He had been born there in Portsmouth harbor, at an inn. Then they had taken ship, with his mother and him following the drum from battlefield to battlefield. And he had never set foot in England. Because his mother was French, that language came as easily to his tongue as the gutter English spoken in the army camps. He could manage French, Spanish and Portuguese better than proper English.

Was Juliet right? Had his father wanted him to return? But to what point? He thought again of his father's traveling chess set. No matter how he tried to play this game, he was always the pawn. First of his father, then Soutine, now Chandler and Juliet. What if he met this grandfather and discovered Cochran wanted to use him as well?

He was sitting at his chamber window with his coat unbuttoned, watching the river, when a carriage pulled up in front of the house and Chandler stepped out. Three menservants accompanied Chandler to the door, which made Gerard feel wary. Now what could he want at this hour except to cause trouble? He would not be admitted, of course. But when Gerard heard pounding on the door and Condé's heavy feet padding down the hall to answer it, he felt once again his life was going to be taken out of his control. He buttoned the fancy dress coat he had worn to the theater, went downstairs to Soutine's room with some notion of protecting him from the persistent man, and was surprised to find him still up and in his wheeled chair.

The old man breathed a heavy sigh. "Who is it?"

"My cousin, Charles Chandler."

Soutine thought a moment, then nodded. "I will see him."

"Do you think that wise?"

"No, but I will see him anyway. Are you going to stand there like an oaf or push me out to the salon? I don't want to treat with him in this sickroom."

Gerard obeyed the command reluctantly. There was nothing like running on your fate when you didn't know what it was to be.

Condé and Chandler were arguing at the door and Soutine spat out a phrase in gutter French that made Condé fall back and admit the Englishman.

"Rather late for a call," Soutine taunted in English better than his own. Gerard turned the chair at the fireplace so Soutine could face the man.

"I want my cousin."

"Open your eyes, then. He is here."

"But what is he doing here?"

"They rescued me after Waterloo. I was knocked senseless." This sounded lame since he could have gone to England any time these two months. Gerard realized Chandler had been drinking. No matter how much he liked his cousin, he would never let him hurt Soutine. He was glad Condé had remained and wondered what he was fumbling with at the corner cabinet? Surely not brandy.

"But why?" Chandler demanded as he took a seat facing Soutine.

It was a question Gerard had asked himself often enough and had never been able to get a plausible answer out of the general.

Soutine breathed a heavy sigh. "Had you seen the charnel house that was laid out on that Belgian field, you would be glad we pulled anyone alive from it. Surely your own soldiers and doctors did nothing for the wounded until the next day. Many died that night for lack of water when they might have been saved. From this springs Gerard's wish to become a surgeon, no doubt."

Gerard knew this for a truth as soon as Soutine spoke it. Why had he not realized it until now? He'd been leaning in that direction, but Waterloo had settled his ambition on him.

"I was not there," Chandler agreed and brushed his hair off his forehead. "Though under other circumstances I might have been."

"So you can have no notion why I did what I did. Suffice it to say that I owe—owed—a debt of honor to Major Cochran, and the only way I could repay him was to save his son."

"Debt of honor?" Gerard asked. He was about to say that Soutine had always insisted *he* was owed the debt of honor but perhaps the old man was just forgetful. Or was the debt just a fiction to hold him?

"Very well. I accept your reason, but the boy must come with me now. He is a British subject. I am here to return him to his rightful home."

"By what authority?"

"He is a minor under the guardianship of his grandfather. I am General Cochran's representative."

Soutine gave a saggy old laugh that ended in a cough. "I don't know that Major Cochran made a will, but if he did I'm pretty sure he would never consign his son to that old tartar."

"No, actually he left the boy's guardianship to Captain Scott, who unfortunately also perished in the conflict."

"So there you are," Soutine said.

"Where?" Gerard asked, never having considered that he might be legally compelled to return with Chandler.

"In Paris," Soutine said, "from which Gerard cannot be moved against his will."

"Does Gerard choose to stay or is he your prisoner?"

Soutine looked toward him and Gerard said, "I choose to remain."

"I don't believe you. We can go to court over this," Chandler threatened.

Soutine wheezed again. "Have you any idea how long it would take a French court to adjudicate the matter? Besides, Gerard is not a child. He is nearly nineteen."

Gerard glanced at the old man with the veiled expression. So he had read the documents in the money belt.

"But the military occupation force, if they knew of Gerard's existence, would insist he be returned to be cashiered out. Since he survived, they might even regard him as absent without leave."

Soutine smiled, leaving Chandler in suspense as to why. "Gerard was never a soldier."

"Come now. The son of a major, traveling with the army. He must have enlisted, at his age. I talked to someone who saw him drumming during the battle. He was wounded on the field of battle. How can he not be a soldier?"

Now all their gazes turned to Gerard. "There was a time when I would have joined up, even if only to drum for the unit, but Father would never hear of it. He deceived me about my age. Otherwise I might be dead now."

"That seems a strange start," Chandler said.

"So it always seemed to me, but I think he liked the army life less, near the end, than he had in the beginning. I had always thought him in control, but I see now that he was swept along by a decision he made very early in life."

"Yes, to defy his father," Chandler agreed. "Soutine, why not make it easy on the boy? Release him from your power."

The old man turned his head sideways to regard him. "And what power do I have over you, Gerard?"

He came around the chair to face the old man. "I have never been sure until now, but finally I think it must be love."

"What?" both Soutine and Chandler said in unison.

"You cared enough about my father and me to come for us. I heard Condé calling for Major Cochran on the battlefield." He glanced toward the servant, who still had his back to them. "You have shown me only kindness. Is it so strange that I would repay you with my regard, my care of you?"

"But he is your grandfather's mortal enemy," Chandler insisted.

"*Was* his enemy," Gerard corrected. "The war—all wars, I hope—are over. I wish I had realized that sooner."

"You mean to stay, then, to flout your inheritance, to dash Juliet's hopes?"

Gerard faced Chandler then. "I wish I could do something for Juliet, but I scarcely know her. There is no guarantee that if I went with you I could make her happy. I cannot free her from her trap or if I did she might not thank me for it."

"You would stay with the enemy instead?"

"The enemy? Now *you* are talking like a soldier."

"I will take you with me. I must." Chandler lunged to his feet and grabbed him. Gerard now realized how very drunk he was.

"And I feel I must stay." Gerard turned toward Condé and discovered the servant had not been idle in this interlude but had loaded a pistol and was pointing it at Chandler.

"Condé, no!"

When the hammer clicked, Gerard twisted in front of his cousin, heard a loud report and felt the ball sear his ribs. Staggering back into Chandler, he felt himself dragged toward the door and heard his cousin giving orders to his servants outside. As though in a dream he saw General Soutine struggle up out of his chair in a fog of black powder smoke, then almost fall as Condé rushed to his aid. He could still hear the servant bellowing as two of Chandler's men shut the door and held it closed against Condé's repeated assaults, while Chandler and one servant loaded Gerard into the carriage. Finally the other two propped a stone bench against the door and leaped for the boot as the carriage lunched forward.

Even though the growing wet warmth told him he'd been shot, it had all happened so fast he could not quite believe it. He laid his hand over the wound and felt something sharp in his side but he did not feel like he was dying. Unaccountably, he started to laugh at how fate had played this hand. Leave it to the knight to surprise you. He wasn't sure anymore if he was the king or only a pawn. It would be interesting to see how the game played out.

****

Juliet peeked under the pad covering the wound on Gerard's left side and pressed it back in place when she saw it had stopped bleeding again. It seemed that every time they helped him out of the coach at an inn to eat or use the necessary, the wound broke open again, but not this time. Perhaps it was starting to heal. After a night, a day, and now another night on the road, Gerard was the only one who had gotten much sleep.

She did not think the bullet was in him but had glanced off his ribs. Still, the gash looked ugly and the swaying of the carriage made it hard to hold him on the seat, so she had stationed herself on the edge of the seat where he lay. Charles sat opposite her with his head craned out the window, looking backward down the road from whence they had come, though how he expected to see pursuers in the middle of the night she did not know. Her maid, Sophie, was sniffling in the other corner from Charles, still terrified by their hasty and desperate departure from Paris.

Her brother pulled his head back in, his hair ruffled from the wind. "How is he?"

"Unconscious again, and he feels hot. Can we not get him a doctor when we reach Calais?"

"No, nor let anyone know he is wounded."

"They're going to see the bloody shirt." She tucked the blanket tighter about Gerard.

"We'll throw your cloak around him. We must hope we can take ship before Soutine can send word we are making off with Gerard."

"But you said we had the right to take him."

"Yes, but right isn't always recognized, especially in France. Can you wake him? We will be there shortly."

As Charles lifted the leather curtain on the coach and

peered out again, she poured rose water out of a vial onto her handkerchief and mopped the feverish cheeks of the young man, then swabbed his brow. She had not been surprised at their sudden departure, for Charles had warned her to pack before he went out, and he had been drinking. While she had paced the sitting room she had in fact wondered if he was planning the abduction of Gerard and had wrung her hands for an hour while she waited for her brother's return. But to be thrust into a carriage containing Gerard wounded had overset her maid, who fainted dead away. It was left to Juliet to help Charles wrap Gerard's lanced ribs and bundle a blanket about him while the menservants loaded the baggage. What a havey-cavey exit. She had found herself in the midst of the emergency hoping that Charles had remembered to pay the bill.

Gerard remained unresponsive as she heard the wheels of the coach bumping over cobbles. On an impulse, she leaned down and pressed her lips to his. Gerard caught his breath and his eyes fluttered open.

"Est-ce que je suis mort?"

"No you are quite alive."

"Juliet?" He breathed out a sigh of relief. "For a moment I thought I had gone to Heaven."

"No, just as far as Calais. Do you think you can stand?"

"I'm not sure. I feel drunk."

"That was the brandy I forced down your throat," Charles said. "If anyone should stop us, Juliet, tell them Gerard is drunk. As for you," Charles said, turning to the maid who cowered in the corner, "keep your mouth shut or I will throttle you."

"So is this an abduction?" Gerard asked.

"No, a setting right of a wrong," Charles vowed. "You are being rescued."

Gerard chuckled, then groaned. "And we wonder why France and England are forever fighting each other."

Juliet took his hand and chafed it. "Be serious, Gerard. If you say one word you could cause both Charles and me to land in a French prison. Is that what you want?"

"In truth, I don't know what I want," he said, gazing at her as if bemused.

Juliet sensed that Gerard meant to pull himself together, and she could only admire him for being so much more mature than her passionate brother. Indeed, when they reached the port it was well into the morning, and Gerard got out of the carriage almost unassisted, then stood holding onto her arm in front of the inn. Charles helped him inside and demanded a private parlor, glaring at Juliet's maid so she would be still.

Charles helped Gerard to a chair, then went to book passage. Juliet was so distracted watching for her brother out the window she missed the entrance of the waiter until Gerard began calmly ordering breakfast for them. She stared at him as though he had run mad. Finally the waiter left them.

She found herself wringing her hands again now that they had come so far. "You mean to help us? Charles told me how you leaped in front of the gun to save his life. What made you do it?"

"My very real fear that Condé would be taken up as a murderer if Chandler was to turn up dead."

"But you could have been killed and it would have been all my fault."

"Your fault?" Gerard leaned back in the chair with a grunt of pain. "How so? For not controlling your brother? He is older and should be more responsible."

"I guessed what he planned to do and did not stop him."

He shook his head. "How could you?"

Gerard looked up at her and she felt compelled to tell him the truth. "I wanted you to come with us so I could know you better and so you could meet your family, especially your grandfather. There are many who think General Cochran is a hard man, but he does care about us. I know he will show the same affection for you." She sniffed and wiped her eyes.

He reached for her, and she went to sit beside him and grip his right hand. It was no longer cold but firm and warm. Perhaps too warm.

"But I was not killed, so there is no point in despairing. Besides, it would hardly have been your fault."

"Everything Charles does is for me."

"Ah, I see. You are still worried about having to make…" He glanced at the maid. "*Un mésalliance?*"

"No. Like Charles I am in a quake that Soutine will send someone after us before we can embark."

"I don't think he will. Come, sit. You need some good English tea to restore your nerves."

When Juliet looked on his confident, sincere face she somehow lost her fear. And even Charles did not have the ability to dispel all her worries. "Is that what you ordered?"

"Yes but who knows what we will be forced to drink." He gripped her hand again. "You are chilled."

"And you have a fever."

"We make a fine pair. I don't feel all that bad. Capital work with the bandages."

"Be serious, Gerard. Soutine wants you with him, for whatever reason. Perhaps Charles is right, revenge on General Cochran."

Gerard straightened in the chair and threw the cloak off. The sight of the blood-soaked shirt caused the maid to whimper.

"When I told Soutine about you, he said he thought I *should* go with you."

"What? Then why did you not agree to come?"

"In his heart he wanted me to stay with him. Have you never done something against your will because it is the best thing for someone else?"

"No, not yet, at any rate." She could feel her lips tremble and saw Gerard's hand come up to stroke her jaw.

"Don't be afraid. We will escape and I will talk to this dragon of a grandfather. Then we will see what is to happen."

"It's not fair. Just because we are young we have no power over our lives."

"I'm getting tired of that myself. What about you? Ah, here comes the tea, bread, and cheese. Charles had better return if he wants anything to eat."

The waiter had bumped the door open and was backing in with a tray, but before he could turn Juliet leaped up and threw the cloak around Gerard.

The waiter who laid their repast barely gave the sniffing maid a glance. Gerard supposed if anything he thought the girl had been admonished by her mistress. So long as she just cried they were perfectly safe. When Chandler returned, Gerard was eating a slice of bread one-handed and Juliet was peeling an apple for him. The maid ate her portion at a corner table, her eyes wary.

"I found an English packet that can take us aboard but not until tonight."

"Try this tea, Chandler," Gerard suggested. "It isn't half bad."

"So you are resigned to your fate?" he asked as he accepted a cup from his sister and sat down.

"I am content to see what happens next. It's almost like a game of chess. But I cannot promise you I will stay at this Old Stand place forever."

"All I ask is that you come for a visit."

"Agreed, then. What could go wrong?"

They had barely finished their meager meal when they found out. A sharp rap at the door announced the entrance of the harbormaster, who demanded to see their passports.

Charles handed over his half dozen folded papers. "These are for my sister, our servants and me. We can't seem to—"

"*Un moment.*" It took Gerard some effort to slide his money belt out and hand over the passport. Juliet stared at it, probably thrilled to see that it was not blood-soaked.

"*Vous êtes Monsieur Gerard Cochran?*"

"*Je suis.*"

"*Êtes-vous Juliet Chandler?*"

"*Oui.*"

"And I am Charles Chandler. This is Juliet's maid, Sophie Hull. My groom, valet, and footman are in the taproom."

The man asked what was wrong with the girl and Gerard informed him in French that she got seasick and was afraid of the crossing. The official seemed on the point of leaving when he turned. "*Monsieur, vous avez sang sur votre manteau.*"

Gerard looked under his arm and laughed. "*Oui. Mon blessure avez ouvrir une fois de plus. La bataille en Belgique.*"

Charles turned to the man. "Our cousin was unable to travel until now. We are here to escort him home. He was fortunate to have survived the battle."

Gerard waited to see if Juliet or himself would have to elaborate on this.

The man frowned and hesitated, perhaps about to ask on which side he had served. There were many Anglo-French families. But he clicked his heels together and bowed sharply. "*Très bien. Bonne chance.*" He left as quickly as he had entered.

****

Gerard was lying on a ship's cot trying to recall his last voyage. He'd had a father then. Now he did not, but he did not feel alone, either. It was amazing how quickly he had become attached to Juliet and her brother.

When Chandler came into the cabin they were to share, he said, "Thank you for not resisting. But why did you cooperate? One word to the port master and we would have been clapped in jail."

"Chandler, you are like the tide. A person may struggle against you, but eventually you will come in and swamp them."

"Admit it, you are curious about meeting the old man."

"Yes, that too. There is one thing I have to know."

"Name it now that we are underway." Charles stripped off his coat and hung it on the back of the door.

"Are you serious about letting me apply for Juliet's

hand?"

Chandler's brows came together. "What a question! If I say no, it will look like I held her out as a lure to you. If I say yes, it will look like I am using you to curry favor with your grandfather."

"Well, aren't you?" Gerard twisted his head to get a better look at him in the dim light.

"Very well. I am because I want to marry my cousin Melanthe and I need my great-uncle's permission to do that."

Gerard closed his eyes. "I have a feeling this is going to get very complicated."

"As most family matters do." Chandler sat on the bunk and gestured. "If I could bring you home, I thought it would help my suit. But I am resigned to losing Melanthe if I can but keep my sister out of Claude's hands any way it is possible."

"Do you mean the general would find favor with me courting Juliet?"

"Of course he would. That was the whole point of bringing you home, to have you marry Juliet and continue the line."

Gerard cast a wary glance toward his cousin. "I thought you said it was just for a visit."

"Trust me. Once you see Old Stand you will want to stay. The house, the herds, the sheep fields... We also have a grist mill besides the wool mill."

"But you scarcely know me. I could be a good deal worse than Claude."

Chandler shook his head. "Do you recall taking that bullet for me?"

"Vividly. My ribs still burn like fire."

"I think we could say you have proven yourself."

"But what if the general takes a dislike to me?"

"You must study to please him. It isn't hard. Lord knows I've been doing it for two years."

Gerard stared at Chandler. "One more question."

His cousin threw himself down in the opposite bed. "Another question? Where will it end?"

"A boon, then. Promise me that Juliet will never be forced into marriage against her will, not even to me."

"Very well. Now get some sleep and don't die in the night. It would hobble all our plans."

Gerard found himself chuckling again even though it made his ribs hurt.

Chapter Five

"You plan to take him into Northamptonshire right away?" the surgeon asked as he bound Gerard's ribs so tightly he wasn't sure he could breath. He sat on the bed in a suite of rooms in what was for him a rather grand hotel in London.

"Must we wait?" Charles asked. "Is he in any danger?"

"Only from pain or infection. I have removed the ball and some bone chips, but his activities should be restricted for a few weeks."

"So the lead was still in there," Gerard murmured, then took an experimental breath and coughed. "I thought so."

"You might have said something," Chandler admonished.

The doctor started packing his gear. "If I may have your attention, a week of bed rest would be far better than a jostling carriage ride of that length."

"But we must leave tomorrow," Chandler said.

"And he must consult a surgeon when you get him home." Suddenly the man looked Gerard in the face. "Who did you say you are?"

"Gerard Cochran."

"Relation to Major Cochran?"

Gerard felt an impossible flash of hope. "Yes, my father."

"He was a good man."

"Yes, he was." So he had met his father but like all the rest of them had no news of him.

"Very well, hare off to the country if you must. I've no doubt you would disregard my orders to the contrary if I gave them." The surgeon accepted his fee and left.

"We'll leave after luncheon," Charles said.

Gerard groaned and Charles looked abashed.

"Tomorrow," Charles added.

The next morning, Chandler's sturdy valet Higgins and Gordon the footman helped Gerard dress in some of Chandler's clothes, which Gerard thought was kind of them after they'd been forced to ride on top of the coach all through France, not to mention their help restraining Condé. It all seemed above and beyond the call of a valet, a footman, or even the groom who had aided in his so-called rescue. Gerard thanked them warmly and they said it was nothing. Gerard went to the sitting room of the suite and found Chandler was gone—on some business, he supposed—but Juliet was waiting for him.

"What's the verdict?" she asked, her eyes intent as Gerard walked stiffly to the sofa and slid into a seated position.

"You've killed me."

"Do be serious for once, Gerard."

"I lost a deal of claret and a few bones were chipped. Nothing that won't mend in a week or so." He tugged on the neckcloth swaddling his throat.

"So we are fixed here this week."

"No, we leave for the country this afternoon."

Juliet gasped. "My brother is an idiot."

"But lovable."

"He will kill you with all this wracking travel." She

jumped up and began pacing the room, while Gerard swiveled his head back and forth to watch her, which pulled on his stitches.

"I'll mend as well one place as another." He looked around the room as though he was part of a conspiracy and whispered, "Did you post it?"

"Yes, I said I would and I did." She came and sat beside him again. "I took it to the receiving office myself since my maid seems to have lost her senses over all this. I got rid of her by sending her on an errand. We don't need her tattling that I wrote General Soutine you survived this escapade, though I am far from sure of it myself."

"There are worse places to nurse your wounds than in a well-sprung carriage."

"Such as?"

"An oxcart in Spain. I swear the wheels were round only when they started and as they went great splinters peeled off so that every turn of the axle was a thumping torture."

"You were wounded in Spain?" Her hand covered his on the sofa, and he turned his hand to grasp hers.

"No, I tended the wounded, or did what passed for tending them. With no training, I had only the word of the surgeons that I was doing them any good. Giving them water sometimes meant the difference between life and death. Or a bearable death and an agonizing one."

"So your life to date has been one long hardship until General Soutine took you in, and we ruined that."

"'Tis true I have been more comfortable these past few months than ever before. I've had a roof over my head that didn't leak, and a fireplace that didn't smoke, more than enough to eat, and I was learning something.

What will it be like at Old Stand?"

"The roof leaks but only when the rain drives in from the east, and the fireplaces do smoke."

He grinned. "But only when a fire is lit."

Juliet laughed nervously. "Gerard, what if we have taken you away from a safe and comfortable life only to thrust you into a dangerous situation?"

"Dangerous? I assure you I am proof against a little rain or smoke."

"I was thinking only about pleasing your Grandfather." She rubbed her hands together. "I hate it when he rants at me. But there is Claude to deal with as well as his father."

"His father would be who again?"

"Your Uncle Nash."

"Right, but he is the heir then, not Claude."

"Only if you are dead. Claude was the one we were worried about since he is the one Great-Uncle planned for me to marry. He thought I might be able to modify his behavior."

"That's a tall order if he's as bad as you say."

"You mean for a girl."

"For any woman. I'll see what I can do about him."

She stared at him, her brow deliciously puckered. "You're not planning on killing him or anything, are you?"

Gerard laughed. "No. Are either of them likely to murder me?"

"That's the awful part. I don't know." She stood up and paced to the fireplace. "Claude is a brute and a bully, but he's not stupid. Nash is more refined, but he has a nastier tongue, which he uses even on Claude."

"You relieve my mind of at least one worry."

"What could possibly be worse than that?"

"I shall not be bored."

****

In spite of Gerard's repeated assurance that he was fine on the journey from London to Old Stand, Juliet suspected he was in a deal of pain. Why else had he asked Charles to get him a brandy at the last inn where they stopped to change horses? And why had Gerard downed it so eagerly? Now he dozed off and on, always waking with a start.

"Are we there yet?"

Charles turned to him with a weary sigh. "Yes, finally we have arrived. That boundary post marks the corner of Old Stand. We have a mile of river frontage. The rest of the property rises. The lower fields are used for crops and the uplands for pastures."

"I know you said you were in the wool trade, but I didn't comprehend in what measure." Gerard gazed at the pastures dotted with sheep.

"It comprises the bulk of our income. But don't throw that up to Great-Uncle."

"Is he embarrassed by living off trade?"

"Not since Charles handles it for him," Juliet said. "The general supervises the crops. You can talk about wool and sheep. Don't mention trade."

"I'm surprised someone as young as Chandler has been saddled with the business. Why doesn't Nash manage it?"

Charles laughed. "He refused, said he had no interest in it."

"What about the oldest son, the one who died—how was it?"

"Aubrey. Broke his neck over a jump. Don't

mention fox hunting, either," Charles advised.

"Not likely. Is there any other topic I should not raise in conversation?"

Juliet thought for a moment. "Your father, war—any war—the French, of course, and what else, Charles? Help me out."

"Mangel-wurzels."

"What's a mango-whatzel?" Gerard asked.

"Some sort of beet that didn't work here. It doesn't matter. Don't mention them."

"There's the house." Juliet leaned forward, and Gerard ducked his head to gaze at the rambling stone edifice, then sat back with a grunt.

"Will you both teach me about the wool trade—in private, of course?"

"So you mean to stick it out?" Charles asked.

"I simply do not want to appear a complete dunderhead. What is a safe topic of conversation?"

Juliet looked at Charles, and he laughed. "No idea from day to day. Just don't rise to any bait Nash casts your way."

"Wonderful."

Juliet loved the expressions on Gerard's face, the way the corners of his mouth turned up in a smile, the way his brows drew together when they had confused him. And she loved conspiring with him and Charles. It had only been the two of them against the world for so long that she'd had no idea what it was like to have a friend.

When the carriage pulled around the loop of drive, Gerard got out stiffly and staggered a little. Though the brandy had relieved the pain, his head was still spinning even several hours later.

"Your grandfather will be in the estate office this time of day," Chandler advised. "But if you are feeling unwell, I can get them to make a room ready for you."

"I don't imagine he would like putting off our meeting."

Juliet cast a warning glare at her brother but said, "Visit him now if you must, but keep it short. I will see to the room and baggage."

Gerard limped after Chandler along a hallway and toward a set of double doors from which shouting emanated. Just as Chandler was about to knock, the doors sprang open, almost hitting them, and a statuesque woman strode out.

"Aunt Helen."

"Shut up, Chandler," she demanded until they sidled out of her way.

"Well?" called a voice from within.

They walked into the study, and Gerard confronted a man who looked shockingly like his father—aged twenty years. There was the firm jaw, the mouth that could be grim, and those brilliant blue eyes. All he had lost when his father died came back to him in a huge sweep of regret. The eyes that glared at him must have found him wanting, or perhaps the chiseled nose had detected the brandy fumes, for the grim expression grew harsher still.

"So, you are the *boy* who says he is Gerard Cochran."

The coldness of the remark caught him off guard. He didn't know what he'd been expecting, but resentment had not been on the list. "You had better hope so, else Chandler is guilty of abducting a French citizen."

His cousin laughed uncertainly as General Cochran

rose. He was half a head taller than Gerard.

"Well, are you, or aren't you?" The man glared at him, or perhaps at Chandler's coat hanging loosely on his thinner frame.

"I am Gerard Cochran." He was now disturbed by the French accent he had worked on so studiously.

"Can you prove it?" The man picked up a riding crop and began pulling the thong end through one hand.

Chandler stood to attention. "He has papers, sir."

"I asked him."

Gerard cocked his head to one side. The temptation to disprove it ran like lightning through his mind. Did he really want to deal with this tartar on a daily basis? Then Juliet's parting, pleading look came back to him and he tamped down his temper. "How do you suggest I do that?"

"How can you be Gerard? The boy traveled with the British army. He would never have a French accent."

"I spoke French to my mother, who raised me while Father was at war."

The gaze could have roasted him. General Cochran turned and paced to the window. "So you have lived in France with your mother all this time, not been with the army?"

"No. We both traveled with the army, mercenary or English, as the need arose. Her family disowned her for marrying an Englishman." Gerard glanced at Charles and saw his eyes bulge. "She died when I was fourteen."

The general turned and inspected him. "Chandler wrote me you were staying with a French family in Paris after the latest conflict. Why didn't you return to the army?"

Gerard slid a look toward Chandler and saw him

shake his head almost imperceptibly. He tried to smooth the accent out of his voice but it was difficult. "They found me after the battle and healed my wounds. I had never enlisted, and there didn't seem any point in finding the army again. I was no longer a dependent. In fact the army had no responsibility for me after Father's death."

General Cochran's head snapped toward him.

"It was General Soutine, wasn't it?" He brought the riding crop down across the desk and split a piece of parchment in half with the impact.

Chandler staggered backward but Gerard resisted the urge to jump. He was no stranger to loud noises. Besides, he feared that if he moved suddenly he would fall over.

"How did you guess?" he asked.

"He knew who you were and decided to keep your existence from me."

Gerard cleared his throat. "I never interpreted his compassion as anything but good will. He knew my father."

"That is not why he sought you out and took you in." The anger in the words cut like a sword blade.

"Why, then?" Gerard risked asking, ignoring the grimacing Chandler, for he really did want to know. Soutine had never satisfactorily answered that question.

"To spite me."

Gerard laughed. "General Soutine does not live in the past."

"As I do? If you cannot prove who you are, you may as well take yourself back to France."

Gerard turned to Chandler with a smile. "I told you it would be a wasted trip."

"But he has papers," Chandler argued.

"They could have been forged, as Helen has just pointed out to me."

"And we have John's trunk," Chandler said. "There may be some proof in there."

"Very well. We will test him with the contents. I've given orders to put him in the blue chamber. After dinner we will discuss this."

They had both turned to go, with Chandler opening the door, when the rough voice asked, "How badly were you wounded to be still favoring your ribs?"

Gerard wondered what had given him away. "Oh, I recovered from the battle long ago, a head wound. These are Chandler's ministrations. He's not much of a dab hand at the kidnapping business."

The arched eyebrows he expected. It was just such a look as his father had when surprised either pleasantly or not. The crack of laughter he had not anticipated. Perhaps there was something human behind that rough military veneer.

Gerard followed Chandler up the stairs and entered the small chamber where Gordon was laying out clothes for him that were not his own.

"Gordon will serve as your valet," Chandler said.

Gordon bowed. "I hope I will give satisfaction. If not, you can choose someone else."

Gerard sat on the bed with a groan. "I was going to say I am not in the habit of needing a valet, but I see that I do."

"Change for dinner," Chandler said. "I bought you some clothes in London that might fit you better than mine. Tomorrow we will order you some new suits."

"Is there something significant about this bedroom?" Gerard commented as Gordon began to pull off his boots.

"By rights you should have claimed your father's room, but his things are still locked up in there after all these years."

"Ah, putting me there would have been an acceptance, and he doesn't want to do that." Gerard tugged at his neckcloth.

Chandler looked puzzled. "I think he does."

"But he doesn't want to admit it, or perhaps cannot afford to until I have passed his wife's acid test."

"You seem to understand him pretty well already."

"He is a lot like Father—or I should say, Father was a lot like him. I see now why they clashed." He stood so Gordon could slide his coat off.

"See you don't do the same. Move smart, Gordon. We don't want to have them put dinner back because of us."

As Gordon helped him change his clothes and finish his wardrobe by tying one of Chandler's neckcloths for him, Gerard decided that his grandfather had addressed him initially as he would a soldier, moreover a soldier absent without leave and drunk into the bargain. Once he realized Gerard was no such thing, he dropped his military shield and seemed more human. Gerard knew this because his father was always stiffer with the troops than with his friends, though he had no end of compassion for the wounded. So there might be a chance to marry Juliet after all, even if he did not mean to stay here. But if he meant to pursue a medical career with the attendant years of school required, was it fair to hope Juliet would wait to marry him, or for that matter, was it fair to assume she would be content to wed a country doctor or a surgeon who might even follow the army?

Now, he was at a real crossroads. He might have to choose between Juliet and what he thought he ought to do with the rest of his life.

****

Juliet nervously tapped her foot as she waited with the family in the drawing room. When Gerard appeared in the doorway she realized Gordon had worked a small miracle with one of Chandler's neckcloths. Her cousin almost reeled backward when everyone stood to be introduced. In rapid succession he made the acquaintance of the general's much younger sister Emma and her children Melanthe and Jack, and of the disapproving Helen and her son Nash and grandson Claude. Though they were all staring at him, it was Nash who attacked first.

"So this is our little impostor?" he said with that drawl he imagined to be so cultured. To Juliet his voice sounded slurred. She could hear the drink in it without smelling his breath.

Gerard merely smiled. "So this is our little heir apparent?"

Juliet clapped a hand over her mouth to stop a giggle.

"Don't jab at me, drummer boy. You are nothing here."

"Silence," the general shouted. "I won't have this bickering in my house."

"Good, for I am famished," Charles said as he opened the doors to the dining room and reached for Melanthe's hand. She was a delicate girl, very quiet and easily trampled in such a family. It would be good if Charles could rescue her even if he did not love her.

The seating could have been worse. At least Gerard

had Juliet on his left and Charles across the way. At the other end of the table, Nash and Claude bracketed his grandfather like bookends, not an entirely apt simile now that Juliet looked at them. There was some resemblance between Nash and the general, but Claude was shorter and meatier than the other Cochran men. Why had she never noted it before? Perhaps because she could see Gerard comparing them. He looked at her then with a question in his gaze.

Charles began discussing the wool deals he had make in France, and it seemed safe simply to listen to him.

"Do you know anything about the wool trade?" Nash asked Gerard.

He finished cutting a bite of the lamb chop and held it up on the end of his fork. "I know excellent lamb from mutton, and that's the extent of it."

Juliet and Charles laughed, as did Emma and Melanthe. Jack stared, wide-eyed.

His grandfather looked at him tolerantly. "He's young enough to learn, if the teaching becomes necessary."

"What do you know?" demanded Claude, who was emptying his wineglass too regularly for comfort.

Juliet could see Gerard quickly edit out of his qualifications anything that would raise an eyebrow. At least that is what she hoped was delaying his reply.

"Languages, mathematics, history."

"That's useless." Claude took another gulp of wine.

Gerard smiled and it made her stomach flutter with worry. He was going to do something wicked. She just knew it by the way the corners of his mouth turned up.

"I can beat the tattoo. I know all the drumming

signals the officers use for orders."

The general stiffened in his chair and his glare shot across the table like a striking snake.

Charles coughed over a groan.

"Fat lot of good that will do you, drummer boy," Nash said.

"Though I was not a drummer, I did aspire to be one. They are very important, you see."

"How so?" Claude asked.

"They are the army's chief means of communication on the march or in battle. I once heard an officer ask a drummer what the order was he was hearing, and the boy replied, "That's the advance, sir," and took up the beat with his own drum. Without those boys the army would have been deaf and dumb."

Juliet could see General Cochran's mouth quirk in a smile, but it was gone so quickly she might have imagined it.

"You'll forget about the army and not speak of it again," he ordered.

"Very well," Gerard agreed and went back to cutting his food, which he could manage if he held his elbow close to his side.

"I still say it's a stupid occupation."

"Claude, I said to stop talking about it," the general shouted.

She saw Gerard smile with satisfaction after Claude got that reprimand. Perhaps there was more to Gerard than she had realized. For one thing, a reprehensible wit.

His grandfather was a man of few words but he expected the ones he uttered to be obeyed. If Gerard respected that, he might be accepted.

Charles expelled a pent-up breath and Juliet leaped

into the awkward silence. "I have brought Belgium lace for all of us. We'll unpack it tomorrow." Fashions constituted the subject of conversation until the ladies rose to leave the gentlemen to their port.

Gerard watched Juliet depart and felt as though he had lost his best ally. Yet he had to stay with the men. The boy Jack could not be more than twelve unless he was undersized, and he stayed and was given a ration of port. The lad had been staring at him, and Gerard sent him a sympathetic look that drew a smile in return.

"Let's get our cards on the table," the general said. "There is no proof that you are Gerard Cochran."

Nash looked smug after that statement.

"I fancy there is a strong family resemblance in my favor." Gerard glanced toward Claude.

It was as though an ember lit behind Nash's gaze and burned under his dark brows.

General Cochran hesitated as he poured the port and a bit dribbled on the cloth. "All will be proven or disproven in good time."

"After dinner we'll have the trunk down, right, Uncle?" Charles asked.

"What trunk?" Nash asked.

"John's trunk was sent home by messenger. It's locked in his room. Can you describe it, boy?"

"He had three. Two large wooden ones with iron bindings for saddles, horse gear, boots, and weapons. The third was well-oiled leather and held his uniforms and personal items. My trunk was a small wooden thing. I never thought to carve my initials in it as he had done."

"Which one arrived?" Chandler asked.

"His personal trunk. I've received a communication from my solicitor in today's post and he wants to be here when the trunk is opened."

Charles took a sip of wine. "Well, when is he coming?"

"He isn't sure. He'll let us know."

"Perhaps Gerard can just tell us about his father," Chandler suggested, "as proof of his identity." He looked at Gerard in a speaking way.

"I could, but if General Cochran does not want to hear about the war, there would be little left to tell. My father was a great and courageous man who followed his convictions and his heart into a hopeless battle that had to be fought and won—if not by him, then by those who did survive." There was dead silence after this speech, and Gerard was not surprised that no one could quarrel with it. Even Nash looked sad. Was it possible he cared about his brother?

"Where is he buried?" the general asked.

"I do not know, sir," Gerard whispered almost as a groan.

"Here now," Claude complained. "Why doesn't he call you Grandfather if he's Gerard?"

The general turned to blast him. "Because he has not been given leave to do so. Must be an element of the army training that rubbed off on him. He at least does not forget anything I tell him or flood me with inane comments."

Chandler looked surprised at this defense of Gerard.

The scrape of General Cochran's chair signaled the end of their male isolation, and Gerard shot the rest of his port down his throat before rising. He had a feeling he would need the fortification.

Chandler walked with Gerard to the sitting room. "I think he likes you."

Gerard coughed. "Is that good? You and Juliet are so normal. I begin to wonder if I really do want to be associated with the rest of these people."

"You'll get used to them."

Gerard glanced over his shoulder but it made his side hurt. "Doubtful."

"How are the ribs?"

"Aching like the devil, but the port should help."

Juliet breathed a sigh of relief when the men entered and there did not appear to have been "blood on the table" as Gerard had termed it. She did not even detect a simmering argument, but no one was joking or smiling, not even Charles and Gerard. Though Juliet was exhausted from three almost sleepless nights, she went to the pianoforte and began to play quiet music that would not prohibit conversation but might encourage it to remain sanguine.

Charles came to turn the pages for her as he usually did, leaving Gerard to sit between his grandfather and grandmother in the only available place open, the middle of the sofa along the south wall. Helen's grim smile did nothing to alleviate what Juliet thought must be a stab of agony in his side but he smiled even if it was in a pained way. His face was so vital usually, showing every emotion, that pretending to be enjoying himself must be a terrible strain. Oh, why had they brought him to this house? If it was not a nest of vipers, it contained a least two men and a woman who would enjoy seeing him dead.

She played as she glanced around at them, cataloging their sins. Emma and her children on the opposite sofa had the least to answer for. Emma and Melanthe were absolute doormats. Poor Jack was forced to sneak around for his own preservation. The general appeared to rule with an iron hand, but Helen often countermanded his orders with impunity. Juliet knew she had tried to stop them from going after John and Gerard, presumably because of the danger. But she was the general's second wife. Nash was her son and Claude her grandson, so it made sense that she would not want Gerard found.

Nash and Claude occupied the armchairs near the chess table, opposite the pianoforte. They were engaged in quiet conversation...or perhaps argument, not to say conspiracy. She played everything she could think of 'til she heard the rattle of the tea tray in the hall, then ended with an almost military flourish that brought a dent to her great-uncle's brow.

Gerard applauded by clapping his free right hand against his left without moving his left arm from his side. When his appreciation fell into dead silence, he said, "Sorry, is it not the custom to applaud in a private salon in this country?"

"Perhaps it should be," General Cochran said and added his applause. The others followed suit. Juliet was so stunned that she rose and curtseyed to the family. Only Helen had ever complimented her before on her playing, and then only in private and not very sincerely.

She decided to get a cup of tea, and seeing that Gerard had none yet, poured one for him. Her great-aunt had left the sofa to pour tea at the large circular table in the middle of the room so Juliet sat next to Gerard for a moment. "I guessed you might like milk and sugar."

"You read my mind. They were such scarce commodities on campaign that we indulged ourselves whenever we could." He took a sip. "This tea is excellent. You must have missed this while you were in France looking for me."

"Seems such a small comfort."

"Made great by the lack of it. Mother always stood by her coffee, bitter and black, but Father loved his tea."

"So you had a home life after all, and memories of them."

"A short one, but family is family even if they gather in a tent or a hovel."

"When did your mother die?"

"When I was fourteen. She died in childbed in Spain. The other women did what they could for her, but she was too delicate to have been following an army train, or so my father said. His one great regret was that he could never make a home for her."

"She could have lived here."

Gerard shook his head. "General Cochran refused, though possibly he had no idea there was no other home she could go to."

"You said her family disowned her as well. Who are they?"

"I have no notion, nor do I wish to know. Another pack of relatives to resent. What would be the point?"

"You seem to be getting on well with your grandfather."

"You were right, Juliet. I find I cannot hate him after all. He is too much like Father."

"I knew you would change your mind. You are one of the most kindhearted men I have ever met."

"Me? What have I done?"

"Saved my brother's life."

"Oh, that. I find I am compelled to like Chandler." He finished the tea and she took the cup from him.

"Let me get you more."

When Juliet rose, Helen sat down by him. "You seem to have a fascination for Juliet." She had a way of lilting her sentences up on the end as though questioning everything. "I thought I should warn you that she and Claude are to be married."

"Are they now? I keep feeling that I should somehow apologize to you for not bringing my father with me. If the general has lost a son, so have you."

"You cannot know all the family history, then."

"How so?"

"I am not John's mother. She died when John was little. I am Cochran's second wife. Nash is my only son."

"Yes, of course. But a stepson is still a son, or should be."

She frowned and aged her face ten years in an instant. "It won't wash, you know, pretending to be Gerard." She said it so sweetly no one else in the room would know how she was trying to rout him. "There are a thousand things to trip you up."

"If I may remind you, I did not seek the family out. Chandler saw me by chance at the theater and noted the family resemblance."

"I'm sure he did and cooked up this plot between you to defraud the family. Juliet must be gullible to be drawn into such a ruse."

"Do not attribute to others a skill for subterfuge that you may find closer to home."

"What is that supposed to mean?"

"I think you take my meaning quite well," he said gazing at the awkward Claude, who stood a head shorter than his father.

"Claude's mother was big-boned."

"Then the portrait of her on the stairway is savagely inaccurate." When he got the guilty start from her he expected, he got slowly to his feet. "It has been a long day. I bid you *bonne soir*."

Chandler followed him out. "What the devil did you say to Helen? Her cheeks are flaming."

Gerard chuckled. "She accused me of being an impostor and you of perpetrating a hoax. While you are watching your back in this house, make sure she doesn't serve you any food others are not consuming."

"Helen? You must have got it wrong."

"Chandler, I can handle the likes of Nash and Claude."

"You can?"

"But insidious women worry me. It is so hard to act against them. You have to wait for them to trip up, but she will. She is too convinced of her own righteousness."

"Helen? And what experience have you had with insidious women?"

Gerard paused with his right hand on the finial of the balustrade. "There were many of them after my father. I bid you good night. What time is reveille?"

"Some of us rise early to ride out and inspect the farms. Helen's brood lies abed 'til luncheon, which is the first meal of the day. Don't worry, you won't be expected to ride." Chandler turned to go back to the salon, then hesitated. "You can ride, can't you?"

"Yes and I can drive a team of six if it comes to that. I may not have been in the army, but I did learn a thing or two."

Chapter Six

Since Gerard slept late the next morning and Gordon had the kindness not to wake him, he missed the morning ride. The last thing he needed was junketing about on a horse. He requested a bath plus the inevitable rebinding of his ribs, which Gordon did better than the doctor.

He found out Gordon was a veteran, wounded at Talavera, hence the slight limp. When he returned unfit for farm work, General Cochran had found employment for him as a footman. Gerard was not unmindful that if he was accepted as the heir, Gordon's fortunes would rise with his own. Likewise if he disowned his new family, as he had half a mind to do, Gordon would be forever a footman.

And here he was thinking he would lose only the friendship of Juliet and Chandler if he left Old Stand. More depended on him than he realized. And if Helen would risk warning him off in the middle of the drawing room, what would she not dare for her progeny outside the observation of others?

And then there was Juliet's hand. He eased his way down the stairs around ten o'clock and heard music from the salon. It wasn't the general who planned to compel Juliet to marry Claude. It was Helen. How could he make his grandfather see that was a mistake and unjust? How could he expose Helen as a harpy when she in no way looked the part? She was fair and sweet-faced. She hardly looked old enough to be mother to a grown man and a grandmother to another, unless she frowned. He had seen enough plays to compose in his mind a scenario for exposure but it must be done subtly. And now he had time, a week at least.

That reminded him of his morning errand. He entered the salon, nodded toward Juliet, and made for the desk. The music stopped.

"What are you looking for?"

"Paper and ink. There is none in my room, and I left France in such a hurry my portable writing desk remained behind."

She came to find the items he required as he seated himself at the small escritoire tucked in the corner of the room. "That's an understatement. You left France with only the clothes on your back, and those were ruined by the bullet. How are we to get you some new ones? Your current wardrobe is most ill-fitting."

"A bolt to the village, that last one we passed through on the way here. I want to mail my letter anyway." He spoke even as he wrote to Soutine, apprising him of the contentious family that he must set to rights before he returned and asking for his baggage. "Have I got this direction correct?"

Juliet looked over his shoulder and said," Yes, but will he send your things?"

"Why not?" Gerard smiled with a confidence he was far from feeling. The letter had one purpose only. Like the missive Juliet had posted from London, it was to let Soutine know he was all right. Nothing else mattered as much as the old man's welfare and peace of mind. As he melted sealing wax and pressed a coin into the hot liquid, he realized he missed Soutine and Condé almost as much as he missed his father. He would have to go back, but not just yet. He had his grandfather to study and one or two puzzles to solve. Not to mention winning Juliet if she would have him.

"And what do you mean about setting this family to rights?"

"Why, Juliet, you were spying on my letter. Come, walk with me to the stables. If no grooms are about, I can hitch a gig myself if only there is a pony or horse."

She ran upstairs for some pin money and a shawl and bonnet. He hoped she would not drag her bothersome maid along. In fact, he did not think there would be room for her in the gig. Gerard pocketed the letter and extracted some guineas from his money belt. He wore it always now because it reminded him of his father.

When Juliet ran back down, she was alone and took his good arm to stroll with him to the stables. The head groom, Conrad, looked dubious when he received Juliet's request for a gig and horse since he knew the state of Gerard's ribs. Gerard assured him he could drive such a small conveyance even one-handed but sympathized with Conrad's intention to send a groom with them. Perhaps it was not the thing in England for a young man to drive his cousin even as far as the village unchaperoned.

While the horse was being hitched, Gerard walked down the line of half doors and found—to his utter shock—Tully mucking out a stall. He suppressed a gasp and said, "We'll take this groom with us."

Tully gaped at him and shook his head no.

Conrad came and shook his head as well. "He's lame and half blind. He may be a war hero to hear him tell it, but he'll be no use to you if the horse bolts."

Gerard took a closer look at Tully and realized he had been wounded again and more than once. "Still, I want him for my groom. I'm sure no one will object. What's your name, soldier?"

"Tully," the old batman said with a sour look.

Once a cob was saddled as well, Gerard helped Juliet into the gig and took the reins one-handed as Tully mounted.

"Should you be driving?" she asked.

"Probably not," Gerard said.

"I'll drive." Juliet took the reins.

They were not even down the driveway when Gerard said, "It's safe to talk in front of Miss Chandler, Tully."

"Then may I ask what the devil you are playing at? If the old tartar finds out I was yer father's batman, he won't just fire me, he'll have me strung up by my...thumbs."

"So you were the messenger who brought the trunk," Juliet concluded.

"Yes, and very distraught I was too, thinking them both dead. I heard Gerard disobeyed orders and left Brussels for the battlefield."

"I had to look for him, Tully."

"And you didn't find him, just as I failed to find you. Where the devil have you been all these months?"

"It's a long story. Suffice it to say Juliet and Chandler came looking for me."

"And they found you, didn't they? So what do you mean to do?"

"Just trying to decide if I want to lay claim to these people as relatives."

Tully coughed. "They do be a quarrelsome lot, present company excepted."

"Thank you, Mr. Tully," Juliet said. "This makes everything so simple, Gerard. Tully can prove up your claim to be Major Cochran's son."

"But I don't want him to. That would end the game far too soon."

Juliet stared at him. "What are you babbling about?"

"Chess," supplied Tully. "Whatever you do, don't play with Gerard."

He turned in the seat and said, "I take it from your presence and Gordon's that Grandfather will support any former soldier but have nothing to do with anyone still in uniform."

"That's the size of it."

"How is that significant?" Juliet asked.

"Don't you see, my sweet? Grandfather is a sham. He has a heart of gold but would die rather than let anyone know."

"What did you say?" she demanded.

"He's a sham, a growl without a bite."

"No, be serious. What was that part about 'my sweet'?"

"But, Juliet, I thought we had an understanding. After all, you did come to France looking for a husband, to which end I was spirited away to this den of insanity."

Tully's crack of laughter was overridden by Juliet's outraged, "What? At this moment I understand nothing."

"But you wanted me to return and marry you to save you from Claude."

"I did that to save your life and bring you back where you rightfully belong."

"Oh, you were not serious, then?" Gerard thought he

faked disappointment well.

"I…am speechless."

"Well, if you don't want to marry me, that's all right, but I still think Claude would be a poor choice."

"I have no intention of marrying him either."

"Then I must warn you that Helen is set on it."

"She's never said anything to me."

"She said something to me."

"Such as?"

"Don't come between you two or she would be shut of me with or without aid of legal counsel. I wonder if the solicitor is in her pocket."

"'T would be my guess," Tully said. "One of the grooms carried a letter to post addressed to a legal firm in York, her birthplace."

"How do you know all this?" Juliet asked.

Gerard shrugged and answered for Tully. "Servants always know more than anyone. The plot thickens. Tully, where can I post this letter?"

"The inn at Sudborough. Have you money?"

"All that was in Father's belt," Gerard said.

Twenty minutes later, Juliet pulled the gig up at the inn and handed the reins to a groom. Tully helped Juliet down and looked not at all surprised when Gerard handed him a coin to post the letter and a guinea for himself. "Get yourself some new clothes, but don't drink yourself into a stupor while we shop for shirts for me."

"Not likely. Try not to start a brawl. I'm not as spry as I used to be."

****

Gerard noted it was a little past noon when they returned to Old Stand. Tully left them and their packages at the front door, tied the cob he had ridden to the back of the gig, then drove it around to the stable. Gordon came out the front door and relieved them of the goods. "Your grandfather was beside himself at your disappearance."

"But Conrad knew where we went."

"As I found out when I inquired. Fortunately no one noticed Miss Chandler was also absent."

Their tardiness was not much remarked upon since luncheon appeared to be an informal meal served from the sideboard in the dining room whenever the members of the family wandered in and took what they wanted. But Helen saw them enter together and glared. Chandler looked up in relief, and General Cochran stared at them but said nothing until Gerard and Juliet had served themselves and taken seats.

"Where the devil were you?" he demanded.

"Sudborough. Repairing my kit. I came away from France with almost nothing, so I have laid in a store of shirts and neckcloths. I shall have to wait for the other clothes to be made."

Nash looked dubious. "You ordered clothes in the village?"

"Yes, they have a respectable tailor. I have always found it wise to patronize local craftsmen. It leaves a better taste." Gerard glanced around the table with a smile. At least four people felt they had been insulted but could not quite figure out how.

"Where did you get the blunt?" Claude asked.

"I did not borrow from Juliet, if that's what you're thinking." Gerard buttered a slice of bread one-handed.

Chandler laughed but tried to turn it into a cough.

The general stared at him, then turned back to Gerard. "I suppose I should make you an allowance so you do not run into dun territory while you are here."

"No need. I'm flush. I say, is that fresh salmon?"

His grandfather gave him a hard look. "If you are flush, you are the first Cochran to say so."

He let this tacit acceptance of his paternity pass without note until his grandfather had taken a bite, then said, "I've told Conrad I'll have that Tully fellow for a groom if no one else wants to lay claim to him."

"Why on earth would you want him?" his grandfather was provoked into asking.

"I saw him in Spain, once, throw his leg over the nastiest horse in the regiment and it listened to him as though he had raised it from a colt."

General Cochran chewed for a moment in thought. "But he's lame now."

"He has a way with horses. Anyway, I've hired him and paid him his first wages, so if this all comes to naught I plan to carry him away with me."

The general stared at Gerard as though he had run mad.

Gerard looked up at him and grinned. "That goes for Gordon as well."

At that the old man's head snapped up. "That you will not. Gordon was raised here as a boy. He won't want to leave."

"If he doesn't, fine, but I've gotten used to him, so I will make the offer."

"Pretty managing for a pretender," Nash said.

"I'm of an age when I *should* be managing for myself." Though he addressed Nash his gaze flicked toward Claude, who was demolishing a dish of eggs.

"What?" Claude asked.

"Nothing, Cuz." Gerard saw in Claude a flicker of

the future he might expect for himself if he let others control him. He should be managing for himself. He should go to London and get a job in a hospital until he had enough money for the education he needed. Of course if he did that, he would not need a groom and a valet. And he certainly would not be able to support a wife.

"Here, I don't like you calling me Cuz."

"You're right, Claude. You have not given me leave to call you anything."

Well," Chandler said. "What's on the agenda for this afternoon?"

"Tour of the estate," Nash said. "If our French *cuz* is up to it. Father has put me in charge of his English education."

"Oh, why not?" Gerard said. Perhaps his grandfather was not as secretly benevolent as he was thinking. He might have given Gordon and Tully jobs out of duty rather than sympathy. To put Nash in charge of him might be worse than being captured by the French. But on the other hand, that had already happened to him.

When Tully brought the black beast out for Gerard, Juliet said, "No. Absolutely not. He can't ride that horse. We need a gig."

"Trust me, Juliet. If Tully thinks I can handle him, it will be all right."

"I wish I was half that confident," his groom whispered. "I've had words with this brute, but he'll try to take you under a limb or else break your leg on a tree. If you've a mind to ride him, stay out of the woods."

"I take it Nash chose my mount for me. Thank you for double-bitting him."

"What good will that do if he's dangerous?" Juliet

asked, examining the double rigged horse and realizing for the first time that the general always rode his mounts this way.

Gerard saw her scrutiny and explained. "A lot of military horses are so hard-mouthed they need the curb bit for stopping and the snaffle for steering. It will be fine."

"Is she right?" Tully demanded. "Should you not be riding?"

"Just a glancing scrape to the ribs on our departure from France."

"Glancing?" Juliet said. "They had to dig the bullet out."

"You never could stay out of trouble," Tully accused.

"Are we going?" Nash demanded from the other side of the stable yard.

"Just mounting," Gerard said as Tully helped Juliet up onto her mare.

"If Wagram has a choice, he turns to the left," the man advised. "I shall be right behind you."

"Which is the safest way to go?" Juliet asked Chandler as Gerard struggled up onto the tall black.

"Oh, I thought we'd go through the home wood," Nash said.

"Woods. Wonderful," Gerard said.

"You must not do this, Gerard. You could die." When she looked over at him, he shook his head and smiled.

"Tully's right. I never can stay out of a fight." He took one set of reins in each hand and that seemed to settle the beast for the moment.

She hoped he had the braking reins in his good hand.

Chandler rode up to him on a large nervous bay. "Are you sure you are fit for this? You can always cry off."

"And leave Claude to bore sweet Juliet to death?"

"Sweet Juliet?" Chandler raised an eyebrow.

She saw the other men string out three abreast and trot down the drive. Gerard started out between her and Chandler, with Tully and another groom behind.

"You did give me permission to court her."

"Have a care what you say in front of the others."

"Chandler, how can you be the most courageous man on earth in the wilds of France, abducting me and carrying me at great risk out of the country, yet fear our Claude?"

"You have not had a taste of his temper. He is my age, yet until I attained my current height, he could beat me to a pulp."

"But how did he provoke you into fighting?"

"By using me against him," Juliet said. "Claude may have inherited Nash's intelligence if not his subtlety."

"I see. Don't fly my flag as your champion unless I can truly protect you."

Juliet had been studying Wagram's head tossing and teeth gnashing. She galloped ahead and whispered to the general. He turned his stately gray and came around to ride beside Gerard. Chandler moved up to Juliet's side. She hoped General Cochran would rescue Gerard this time from his foolish pride.

"Are you sure you can handle old Wagram? He must be twenty if he's a day."

"He has been thinking himself retired," Gerard said.

"Yes, how did you guess?"

"The usual progression for a battle horse who

survives."

His grandfather cleared his throat. "You can turn back and choose your own mount."

"I am more used to playing the hand fate deals me."

Juliet knew this for a truth. Gerard just seemed to accept whatever happened to him.

"Or Nash?" the old man asked.

"Why did you put him in charge of my repatriation?"

"It was Helen's idea. She thought it might help you get to know one another."

Gerard laughed. "I'm sure she's right."

Juliet thought this was going to be the worst ride of her life, and she did not see what she could do to stop it. Was this what the wives of soldiers felt, this utter helplessness in an emergency? It wasn't that she didn't want to pick up the pieces when Gerard failed. It was that she didn't want him to fail. And she realized she was being unfair because she didn't even want him to try. He had asked her to trust him, and she should, but that didn't mean she would not still be terrified for him.

Gerard paid attention when they paused at the overlook before the drive descended to the woods. Nash pointed out the stud farm to the east and the sheepfolds and storage barns to the west. Some of the tenant cottages along the road were also visible from the vantage point.

"Good ground," Gerard said.

General Cochran slid a glance his way. "Do you mean that in the military sense?"

"What? Good ground to defend? The place *is* called Old Stand. But I was speaking agriculturally."

Then Gerard saw it, the slightest twitch of the old

man's mouth. His grandfather had a sense of humor, perhaps a reprehensible one, but there it was. It was the sort of thing that reminded him of his father.

Then Nash gave the office to lope, and Wagram almost shot from under him. Gerard pushed aside all his careful dressage lessons and recalled their wild escapes in Spain on his father's string. He had the reins for the curb bit in his right hand and was able to keep the beast to a jog. He should ask Tully what had become of his father's horses.

As his groom had predicted, Wagram veered left toward a tree and only by pulling on the snaffle reins was he able to avert a collision with a branch. He circled the horse and came up behind the others. Wagram then sidled in his canter toward a large beech on the left. So Gerard had to use his right arm to manhandle the horse to the right. Tully growled at the brute and the great black ears flicked about as the beast staggered back onto the path.

He kept telling himself he had the power to control the horse, he just had to be willing to use it. The others were cantering ahead except for Juliet and Tully, who hung back to observe his struggle. Gerard feared some injury to those near him, so he sprang Wagram and let him do what his heart demanded, lead.

Once he had passed the others, the horse became calmer. Unfortunately Gerard had no idea where he was going. The hoofbeats that approached on his right turned out to be Nash. At least his uncle could ride.

"You are off the main track," Nash shouted.

Gerard slowed the horse and turned it to the left in a wide arc where the woods were more open. Wagram made another feint at a tree trunk and Gerard cursed in

French as the stitches tore in his side. This was altogether not working. But he brought the beast around and rejoined the family on a more pronounced track. With unfortunately one overhanging limb. But he was ready and growled in the stallion's ear as he ducked. This spooked the horse and almost impelled him into the back of General Cochran's gray.

Finally they made it to the main road with Wagram fighting the bits ferociously.

Nash turned an amused eye on him. "Perhaps you should walk him."

"Or we should turn around," Juliet said. She looked terribly frightened, and no demonstration of competence was worth one moment of worry or fear for her.

"No, I simply must have a discussion with this horse. No need to wait for me," Gerard said as he rode the beast back toward the home wood and straight at a tree.

With a warning growl he turned the horse to the right by force, throwing it on its side. He hopped off as the horse struggled to right itself but jumped back on and found his stirrups as the beast struggled up and shook itself. The sound of Gerard's laughter must have come as a surprise to it and all of them.

He repeated the maneuver once more, this time omitting throwing the horse down, and the animal obeyed the right turn when Gerard growled in his ear. Then he relaxed the reins and let Wagram get within crushing distance of a trunk. Another growl and a kick in the flank scooted the beast back into the track. Finally Gerard galloped back to them and stopped the lathered horse with still some bit jiggling but more control than before.

"Are you finished?" his grandfather asked less in irritation than amazement.

"For now. I rather like this old brute. I think I shall always like to ride him."

"Why on earth?" demanded Juliet. "He just tried to kill you."

"Ah, but we have an understanding now. At least I know what this enemy is apt to do, and we have a truce of sorts."

General Cochran shook his head, and they went west up the road toward the cattle barns.

Gerard could feel blood sticking his shirt to his ribs, but the joy of beating Wagram to a standstill made him feel so good that the stabbing in his side could be ignored to some extent.

Taking the lane around the western perimeter of the estate, they passed the sheep fields where all the stock was out at pasture, dotting the green hillside with white. Finally the party rode back at a tired trot along the lane. They were dismounting in the stable yard when Nash stared at Gerard.

"There is blood on your shirt," he said in an undervoice.

Gerard looked down where his coat had gapped open and laughed. "What do you care so long as it isn't yours?"

"But how were you injured? I did not see you crash into anything."

So he had not been told. "If you must know, I was shot by my own servant during Chandler's abduction of me from France."

"What?" Nash squeaked.

Gerard handed the reins over to his groom. "Tully,

cool Wagram down and feed him well. We have reached an understanding and I plan to ride him always."

"I thought you might," Tully said as he took the reins and turned the horse to walk him. "By the way, there's blood on your shirt," he said out of the side of his mouth.

"Yes but don't mention it to Juliet…or Chandler, for that matter. They feel badly enough already."

Tully nodded and led the horse away to cool it.

Having Nash follow him into the house on his heels was disconcerting for Gerard. Could it be that the man was not the villain he'd supposed?

"But did Father know about this?"

Gerard turned at the base of the stairs. "Yes, why?"

"And he said nothing to keep you from riding?"

"No blame will attach to you, if that's what you are thinking, though to be following your mother's promptings toward bringing about my ruin is not well done of you. The general will respect you a good deal more if you take your orders and your tone from him."

This left Nash gaping at him from the foot of the stairs while he marched up them to face the recriminations of Gordon. After this dedicated individual had cleaned his side and bound his ribs again, Chandler broke into the room. "Is this true? Your wound opened again?"

"Just tore two if the stitches. It will mend, but it's too late to have it sewn again. Who told you anyway?"

"Nash."

Gerard frowned at him. "I hardly expected him to care."

"He wants you proved an impostor. He doesn't want to kill you."

"Are those his words or your guess?"

"His words and I believe him."

Gordon excused himself to carry the bloody basin away.

"So it's Claude who is my next worry. Tell me about him."

"His mother died giving birth to him. She was always in delicate health."

"That could turn a child. I can't see Nash choosing a sickly wife."

"Nash was very wild until Helen arranged for him to marry a London miss against his will."

"A girl his mother chose? How could she force him to do that?"

"By withholding money from him."

"The general knew that?"

"The general found him uncontrollable as well."

"Nash must have hated the whole situation."

"Yes, he could never get on with Diana. I think that's why he spent so much time in London. She was fragile, too fragile for Nash. Helen raised Claude."

"That explains much."

"You are here now. The general likes you. Does it matter?"

"It matters if Claude's expectations are still to rule Old Stand someday. We need a plan."

"We need a great deal more than a plan. Nash tried to unseat you with guile. Claude won't be so gentle. Perhaps Juliet is right. We have risked your life to buy us our security."

After a sharp rap, the door opened and General Cochran strode into the room. He surveyed the bloody clothes and bandages and gave Gerard an assessing look. "Do you want us to send for a doctor?"

"No need. Gordon has done everything I require."

"In your estimation."

"I spent a deal of time with the wounded and do know what I am talking about in this case. I will be fine."

"Very well." The general turned at the door and looked from one to the other of them. "Carry on."

The door shut behind him and Chandler once again expelled his pent-up breath. "Do you suppose he heard us?"

"Of course he heard us," Gerard said. "He's probably laughing his head off in private."

"Do you really know what you are about, Gerard?"

"It will be interesting to see if I succeed." Though what he planned to do he could not say. Was he trying to show courage and merely displaying stupidity? It occurred to him he was trying to win more than Juliet's hand. He wanted his grandfather's respect—and Nash's. If he could win Nash over, he might be able to control Claude.

Chapter Seven

Juliet had the news from her maid that Gerard had broken open bleeding again. Sophie had said it smugly as though she knew everything and Juliet was incompetent. It made her wonder if the girl had gossiped to the other servants about their hasty exit from France. No matter how intimately Juliet had nursed Gerard on the voyage home, she felt isolated from him now and worried that he would not confide his hurts to her. But when he appeared in the drawing room before dinner he only moved stiffly, his coat hanging loosely on him as he came to sit next to her.

"What will you do for an encore tomorrow?" she asked. "Get yourself killed?"

"Tomorrow it will rain, so there is no possibility of riding."

"How do you know?"

"Tully told me."

"Tully? What does he know about weather?"

"I think he is right. The wind is from the east." Gerard nodded toward the smoking fireplace.

He surprised a giggle from her. Gerard had a sense of humor about everything.

Impelled by an elbow from Helen, Claude crossed the room and grabbed Juliet's hand, almost dragging her to her feet. The general rolled his eyes and took Helen's arm to escort her in to dinner. Juliet was disappointed.

Until Gerard proved his claim, he was still being relegated by protocol to the status of a poor relation. Less than a poor relation. A pretender.

But the seating ran counter to her expectations. She had the mountain of Claude on one side and Helen on her other as though they were hemming her in. Gerard was next to General Cochran on her side of the table so that she could hardly see him. Charles was studying Claude, and Nash was eyeing Gerard with a dent between his eyebrows. All the Cochran men had it, that mark of concentration between their straight eyebrows. That and the so-charming smile just at the corners of the mouth. Claude had a trace of that smile, but the rest of his face was different. No one would take him for a Cochran. And it suddenly struck her that possibly he wasn't one of them. He was large and purposeful, not lithe and graceful like the Cochrans. What if it was Claude who was the pretender?

When Gerard saw her comparing Nash and Claude he shook his head. So he realized it as well, yet was subtle enough to warn her off the topic. Helen addressed some comment to her and she snapped her head around when she realized the word wedding ended that sentence.

"What wedding?"

"Yours and Claude's"

Juliet dropped her spoon in her soup and the spatter made Helen flinch backward. "There can be no wedding between us."

"Why not? It has been spoken of in the family for years."

"Not by me."

"But you must marry."

"Why?" Gerard asked.

The general cast him a warning look.

Helen gritted her teeth. "That is what women do."

Gerard sent Chandler a speaking look.

"Many an heiress has chosen to remain single and in charge of her fortune," her brother said.

This was not exactly true, Juliet thought. A few heiresses had managed it.

Claude's face was pink, but it may have been the effect of the dinner wine. "Someone must manage her affairs."

"Stop," Juliet said. "I will not be discussed as though I am not here. Charles can manage my business matters or teach me how to do it. If I ever marry, it will be to a man who will not squander my money." She thought about jumping up and leaving the table, but she was hungry *and* she had not been the one to bring up a totally inappropriate topic at table. Instead she turned her head toward the footman as though the matter was closed and he removed her soup bowl.

Only Helen broached family matters in the presence of the servants, and she now seethed at the upshot of opening the wedding item when she might have guessed the discussion would turn nasty. Juliet's cousin Melanthe and Aunt Emma looked terrified. Jack wasn't even present. Gerard looked like he was going to say something, and she shook her head, nailing him with a threatening look.

"So you are not one to miss the main chance," Nash said. "You are waiting to see if the impostor will be recognized before you make your decision. My compliments on your agility, my dear."

Gerard choked on his wine.

General Cochran had gone back to eating, but his

head came up at this and he stared at his son in disbelief. "This is no time or place for such discussions."

"I am only trying to settle matters," Helen whimpered with a good show of tears. Finally it was she who left the table, and no one ran after her, though both of the other women looked toward the general as though awaiting orders to do so. His brows were as black as thunder but he did not rise. Charles finally had the courage to mention the markets.

Now, why had Nash taken the general's wrath on himself? Was he trying to protect his mother? Or to prevent the weeping display that carried her from the room? Juliet had never liked Nash but had always found his reasoning sound though often reprehensible. What game was he playing?

When the fruit and nut dishes had finally made the rounds and the women were clearly finished, Juliet glanced toward her Aunt Emma, who seemed to be in a panic. Then she looked at General Cochran and he gave her a nod. Not Emma but Juliet. It was almost as though he had bestowed the leadership of the household upon her if she wanted it.

"Shall we leave the gentlemen to their port, ladies?" she asked as she slid her chair back. Several footmen leaped forward to assist with the chairs, and Juliet led the ladies out. The others went directly to the drawing room, but she retreated to her chamber.

Angry voices in Helen's wing indicated that matriarch's dresser was paying for the storm at the table. When Juliet got to her room, her own maid was nowhere about. Sophie had been far less attentive since the trip to France and Juliet suspected the girl had a beau on the staff. She found her sheet music and went back down to encounter Gerard in the hall.

"How did you escape?" she asked.

"I pulled out these cigars and got drummed out of the room. The general will not permit anyone to blow a cloud in the house."

"I didn't know you were given to such a habit."

"I am not, but Tully is. I bought them for him. Walk with me to the stable?"

"You bought them to have an excuse to absent yourself and neglected to correct Great-Uncle's assumption." In spite of her accusation, she laid the music on the hall table and pulled her shawl about her.

He chuckled. "You are a clever girl. Sometimes it's what you don't say that is so much more important than what you do say."

"I agree."

"Thanks for giving me that warning glare." He opened the back door for her and picked up a small lantern.

"At least you are capable of taking my meaning from a look. I hope you don't mean to be out past dark." Juliet took the lantern from him so that they could link arms.

"No, of course not. The obvious deduction isn't always the correct one."

"Because I balked and you did not leap in to defend me, Nash bore the brunt of the General's anger. Why did he do it?"

Gerard shrugged. "I fancy that was his attempt to lighten the situation."

Juliet laughed. "It didn't work. At least Helen is the one in disgrace."

"Hmm. I'll wager she doesn't warm Grandfather's

bed tonight."

"I doubt she has warmed it anytime this decade." She whispered now since they were approaching the stable block and the servants had enough to gossip about.

"I see. I was used to loving parents."

"So was I." They glanced around the stalls, but the grooms must have been at supper.

"Why do you suppose he married her?" Gerard asked.

"I always thought she had some money, but I don't know that."

"Somehow I cannot see the general living off a woman. He'd rather starve. I think he wanted more sons."

"Possibly." They walked together along the row of half doors still open. Wagram turned away from them to pout in a corner of the stall, or so it seemed to her. "You must talk to Charles. I think there is much he never tells me."

"You should never be compelled to marry, or if you choose to, find someone who will let you keep your security." Gerard dropped her arm to produce a small apple from his pocket.

"I had always though myself trapped."

Gerard bit the apple noisily. "You have only to say no."

"What did you say to Wagram to keep him from killing you?"

"I growled at him. Tully told me that might work."

"The man is a paragon." Juliet watched as Wagram circled the stall and stretched his neck out to put his lips closer to the apple in Gerard's hand. "Here let me." She took the apple and held it in her open palm. Wagram came and took it without hesitation.

"Tully is probably even now mixing old Wagram a bran mash to ease his sore mouth."

Tully's head popped out of the next stall down the row. "No, I'm not. I'm still mucking. Do you really think you have made your peace with that horse?"

"At least I know how far I can trust him, which I can't say for Helen Cochran." Gerard held out the cigars.

"Bless you, boy. I didn't think you would remember. Let's go outside. If I get caught smoking in here, they'll turn me off without your leave."

They walked out behind the stall to the area where the grooms cleaned harness. Gerard handed him the lantern and Tully lifted the slide to light his smoke.

Juliet laughed. "Not the most obvious use for a lantern."

"Does smoke offend you, lady?" Tully asked.

"No, only being kept in the dark."

Tully led them to a rude bench, and Gerard swept it off to make a place for Juliet, then sat beside her.

"I suppose you want to know about the battle."

"I reckon there is little to tell. You could not find Father either."

"I did look after they patched me up. To tell you the truth, with the amount of carnage I could have walked right by him and not recognized him."

Juliet perceived tears in the old man's eyes. "I'm sure you did your best."

"It's all right, Tully," Gerard said. "I'm sorry. You were as close to him as I was."

"Picked me out of the stews in Plymouth, he did. I hadn't much of a life before then. We had plans for a horse farm someday."

"I didn't know," Gerard whispered.

"As the wars dragged on, he ceased to speak of it. I don't think he figured to come out of that last battle."

Gerard nodded. "That was the impression I had."

"I wish I could have known him," Juliet said, reaching for Gerard's right hand and clasping it.

"He would have liked you," Tully said. "You have spirit like his wife."

"Thank you, Tully," Juliet said. "I think if I had to I could be a soldier's wife."

****

Gerard wondered if they were to be relieved of Helen's menacing presence for the whole evening, but she made an entrance after he and Juliet came in and joined the others in the drawing room. That she regarded him with suspicion was evident from her narrowed eyes. She could ask Claude later and discover that Juliet had been missing during the same time he had. Looking at her critically, Gerard decided she seemed too florid to need the vinaigrette she now clutched.

Juliet took her music to the pianoforte, but Helen made a motion with her hand and shook her head. "Please, no music tonight. I have the headache."

"What do you want to do tonight, then?" General Cochran asked.

"Whist. We have not played in ever so long."

The general rang and had some chairs brought from the dining room. Emma demurred and said she would sew. The table of General Cochran and Helen paired with Juliet and Claude was set up around the central tea table. Chandler took a chair across from Melanthe at the chess table, so Gerard was to be Nash's partner. They sat down opposite each other with a measuring look. "I hope we are not playing for money," Gerard said as he cut the deck.

"In deference to your poverty, we will play for penny points," Nash conceded.

After two hours of whist, Nash and Gerard were the clear winners, sweeping the table again and again. It was as though they could read each other's minds. Helen and the general were swamping Claude and Juliet, but nobody much cared. Gerard was almost sorry to hear the rattle of the tea cart, for he did like to play cards and seldom got the chance.

Chandler threw in his last hand and leaned back in his chair. "Now I am the one glad we are not playing for money. Nash and Gerard would have looted us."

"Where did you get your gift for numbers, Cuz?" Nash asked as he stacked the cards and returned them to their box.

"There are not so many cards to keep track of. Try counting horses or soldiers when they are all moving about."

"Do you play any other games?" Nash drawled.

"Chess."

"Good. We will have a game next time it rains. So what are your other avocations?"

"I am fond of the theater."

"That's not a skill we want to cultivate," Nash said as he took a cup of tea from his mother. "Can't have an actor in the family. Surely you have some gentlemanly pursuits."

"I know how to shoot and kill what I hit. Nothing else comes to mind except one."

"You have us all a twitter," said Nash. "What do you do well?"

"Of necessity I've developed some skill treating wounds and the sight of blood never turns me queasy. I think I could become a fair surgeon."

"Absolutely not," General Cochran said as he rose.

Gerard did not even blink. "And that exhausts my repertoire of skills and ambitions. Tell me, Nash, why you are so interested in finding me occupation?"

"It's not occupation so much as seeing that you don't embarrass the family. Claude already knows what it means to be a gentleman. But you were raised roughshod in the army. There's no telling what you might do in polite society."

Gerard laughed. "I withdraw my objection, then. But I already know how to play cards and drink. What did you have in mind?"

Claude opened his mouth to protest this comment but was interrupted.

"Fencing," Helen said. "Any gentleman must know how to fence."

"I don't think we should tackle that just now," Nash replied.

"Why not?" the woman demanded.

"Our enterprising cousin was shot in the ribs as he escaped France and neglected to mention it to anyone. A fencing lesson will definitely have to wait. I think chess. Tomorrow we begin."

Gerard pursed his lips to avoid smiling. As the party broke up and he walked toward the outside door, Chandler caught up with him. "Now why did Nash let you off the hook?"

Gerard pushed the door open and they walked around the house toward the rose gardens on the west side. "I come to think he is not half so bad a character as

I had at first supposed."

"No, he must have some ulterior motive for instructing you and almost seeming to accept you into the family." Charles walked with him and gazed out over the fields where fireflies lit up the evening.

Gerard shrugged and felt a twinge. "What puzzles me is why Nash is so complacent now when he seemed on the attack before."

"I think I know. He had a long session with Great-Uncle in the estate office this morning while I was working on the books in the library. Only Old Stand and the immediate lands are entailed. The general can leave the rest of the estate as he pleases, including his share of the wool mill, the grist mill and the funds. He and my father were partners in the wool mill. I hope to buy him out when I come of age."

"That would make more sense, really." Gerard stopped walking and turned to him. "In case one of us does poorly, everything won't be sunk."

"You would see it that way. How comes it you have more sense than Nash and Claude together?"

Gerard shrugged. "Perhaps the acumen is inherited. The general did not sell out of the funds when they plunged after the battle."

"How did you know that?" Charles asked.

"Just a guess."

"In his determination to prop up the national economy, he stayed the course, and I did as well. We recovered better than ever."

"If you had the running of your affairs, you would not have sold either." Gerard put his booted foot up on a bench and tried to relax the stiffness in his back.

"It was agreed between us. It was one thing we could

do here to support the war effort."

"You are more a son to him than any of his real sons. It would seem that you should have the running of the wool operation even if he does not mean to sell it."

Charles nodded. "That does not mean he will hand it over to me. I have no desire to live under his command forever, writing his letters, delivering his orders. I could be replaced by a biddable secretary."

"And I am used to taking orders and delivering them. I see." Gerard looked out across the fields and took a deep breath. "Perhaps Nash is waiting."

"For the general to die so he can take over?"

Gerard laughed. "No, for the general to overhaul his staff of officers. Perhaps his father promised Nash something to keep the peace."

"Leave it to you to put a military bent to it. Helen has some money of her own."

Gerard snorted. "I fancy Nash would rather bite off his tongue than ask her for a farthing. He now understands how she was using him."

"Really? For a newcomer, you seem to know a lot about this family."

"When I am quiet I'm not wool-gathering but listening and watching."

Chandler pursed his lips. "It's a game to you, isn't it?"

Gerard let his foot hit the ground and resumed his circuit of the house. "No, this is quite serious, not to mention dangerous. My desire for Juliet is certainly not a matter of fun. Somehow I must help you keep her future safe. She is starting to see that she does have choices."

"Are you hoping that one of her choices will be

you?"

"Only if she is willing. Perhaps she would rather have a season in London. You have to admit she could do better than me, certainly look higher."

Chandler nodded. "Because of her fortune, many of the *ton* would overlook our rise from trade, but that sort of man would make sure he controlled her wealth."

"So we must protect her not just from Claude but from the rest of the world."

"And I fancy that is easier to do here than in London."

"Time enough to decide that if I survive the week."

Chandler rubbed his eyes and followed Gerard. "Do you plan to stay, then?"

"Unless Soutine needs me."

"Why do you feel so tied to him?"

Gerard turned toward him. "When Condé came looking though the battlefield, it was my father's name he was calling. I just rose when I heard it and staggered toward him, hoping we would both find him. I don't think Soutine even imagined I was on the field."

"So the link is to your father, that debt of honor he mentioned. What could it be?"

Gerard smiled. "It was the first I heard Soutine owed him anything, so I have no idea."

"Another little mystery." Chandler pulled out his watch and checked the time in the fading light.

"So is Nash any good at chess?"

"I can't beat him," Chandler confessed.

"Then tomorrow holds some promise of amusement." Gerard turned at the corner of the house and walked toward the front door.

"You forgot to smoke your cigar."

"I don't smoke."

Chandler looked startled, then laughed and followed him back into the house. "I'm two years older but I swear I could take lessons from you."

Chapter Eight

Even though sheets of rain deluged the windows, Juliet rose at her usual early hour and went to the drawing room to practice music for a time. The small fire there failed to knock the chill out of the air, so her fingers soon became too numb to do her much good. When she stopped playing she heard it, a drum beating somewhere softly. She grabbed her shawl and followed the sound to the box room in the basement under the drawing room.

There stood Jack, his left heel tucked into the hollow of his right foot and a drum slung off his shoulder and resting on his left thigh. He began very softly on a long roll of beats, and when he faltered went back and started softly again, each roll getting better and longer and faster.

When Gerard noticed her, he came around and dusted a place for her to sit on a crate.

She sat and stared at him. "I had thought the rain would keep you out of trouble, but teaching Jack any of this is sure to irritate the general."

"Oh, I know, but it has been so long since I angered him I thought it was time."

"You have the most horrible sense of humor."

He shrugged. "I'm not sure where it comes from."

"Gerard, why bring up memories of the war?"

"I don't know. Perhaps it was seeing the drum again."

"What's significant about the drum?"

"Look at the bloodstains. Some of them are mine. It's the one I was beating at Waterloo. The drum from our company. Tully must have found it and brought it back."

"Still, you should try to put all that behind you."

Gerard stared at Jack, who continued to drum. "Another thing that puzzles me."

Even when he wasn't smiling he seemed to be on the point of it. "What?" she asked.

"I would have thought my father and my grandfather would not agree on anything, yet they both enjoyed military life, or so their long careers would imply. So they both must have become disenchanted with war and fighting later in their careers."

"Would not anyone?"

"Anyone not hardened to it. So neither was a professional soldier, a killer by occupation. They each saw it as a necessary and uncomfortable duty."

"I'm sure you're right."

"So why could they not come together?"

"I don't know, and I regret it. If your father had brought you home, he'd be alive and we might have known each other earlier instead of meeting by chance."

He smiled at her. "And yet we were destined to meet. Do you believe in fate?"

"I don't believe in luck for I have had precious little of it."

He bent so close he could have kissed her but he didn't. He just smiled. But Jack, facing the other way, got louder and louder 'til it made her insides thrum.

Gerard turned his head toward Jack. "You've mastered the long roll. Now try camp taps like I showed you."

"What is all this in aid of?" Juliet demanded.

"Jack is bored. Grandfather should let him ride out with the men."

"It is his mother who keeps him from dangerous pursuits, not Grandfather."

"The general should realize riding is not the most dangerous thing the boy could do."

"And you are going to show him that? I can guess what you are planning, and you'd do better to stop right there if you ever want to be recognized in this house."

"But think how much fun it would be."

"No! I refuse to think about your disgrace. I'm going to warn Charles what you are doing."

She got up and left but shut the door firmly, which stifled the sound. She ran up the stairs to check the first floor but only from the drawing room could she hear the drumming. No one went in there in the morning, and she did not tattle to Charles.

Gerard waited for the inevitable boom to fall, but Chandler never appeared so Juliet must not have snitched. After the lesson they packed the drum away carefully and closed the trunk which belonged to his father's regiment. Tully must have brought it back as well. Since Tully had found the drum, it meant that if Condé had not found him then Tully would have, and what would have happened then? Would he have brought him here? It was interesting to speculate, but he was not sorry how things had turned out.

How Jack had found the drum was no mystery. An active boy, housebound because of a timid mother, he was destined to ferret out every corner of an old place like this. They came up the basement stairs together to confront Nash and a carter in the hall.

"It appears your trunk has arrived," Nash said.

Gerard stared at it. "That was fast, unless Condé sent it without hearing from me."

"Well, it is here. I'll have the servants carry it up. Also, I have to find someone to pay this fellow."

"I can do it." Gerard slipped the man a guinea, which was overpayment but he wanted to worry Nash.

The fellow dropped his surliness and ducked into a bow after his profuse thanks, even offering to help wrestle the trunk upstairs.

Nash arched an eyebrow. "You will be spoiling the tradesmen hereabouts."

"But I really appreciate him bringing my clothes."

"Chess lesson at eleven," Nash reminded him over his shoulder as he walked away.

"I shall see you then. Jack, do you want to see what's in here?"

"Of course I do. There could be anything in a trunk."

The boy followed the footman and the carter to Gerard's room, but when the large trunk, which Gerard did not recognize, was thrown open in the middle of the floor it contained many books and his flute but only his court clothes and evening suits. His riding clothes and ordinary coats and hats had been omitted.

Gordon looked at him in despair as Gerard cocked his head. What was he to make of that? Soutine had a reason for everything he did. And it appeared he wanted Gerard's family to think him a fop. Finally at the bottom of the trunk were his fencing foils and equipment, plus a saber. Not his father's, of course. So he wanted Gerard to hide his identity, at least for a while, but arm himself against attack. Gerard had the uncanny feeling that the saber had belonged to Soutine. It was certainly French.

Did this mean he was capitulating?

Soutine would do anything for the sake of a joke. That climate had only enhanced Gerard's own terrible sense of humor, usually to Condé's despair. But without warning he was beset by a memory that went much further back. His mother playing at hide-and-seek with him in a hedge maze and calling to him with a variety of voices. They were at that country house that sat in the back of his mind somewhere as home, but he did not connect the location to his father at all. Certainly there was nothing so frivolous as a hedge maze at Old Stand. Besides, he had never been here before.

He remembered a voice, gravelly and angry, shouting at his mother. Whoever it was had left in a carriage in the dark. Then there came his father to get them and they were constantly on the march. Why they had been separated for a time he did not recall. He remembered his mother had been ill and had recovered on the estate. Once reunited, his parents had been happy and very much in love.

He smiled and tried on the puce coat that Gordon had picked up between two fingers as though it would bite him. Jack laughed at Gerard's posturing and Gordon's grimace. Chess might be more fun than he had supposed.

"Here, Jack, see if you can get a sound out of that flute. If you can, I'll show you how to play the notes."

At eleven Nash's drop-jawed wonder at Gerard's appearance was worth the time it took to change.

"What the devil are you playing at?" he asked as Gerard seated himself at the small chess table in the drawing room.

"What do you mean? Do you want white or black?"

His cousin looked to the board. "You may have white. Are you deliberately trying to provoke my father?"

"I feel like I've fallen into a nest of vipers, you included. It would probably be a wise move to get tossed out."

"It's all about expectations. When someone upsets the applecart, it takes time to adjust."

"Will Claude adjust?"

"He'll have to, won't he?" Nash said as he set out the pieces.

Gerard always felt chess to be a substitute for war, so he played carefully, not allowing any casualties he could avoid.

****

Juliet understood what the drumming that morning had been in aid of, but she had not wanted to broach the subject with Jack present so she came down for luncheon early, hoping to have a word with Gerard. She saw the back of a stranger facing Nash across the chess table, a man in a wine-colored coat. But no. It was Gerard. This could not be any of his English clothes, not with lace cuffs. When she circled the two suspiciously, she found Gerard also wore a lace jabot. He looked like a dandy. What was he thinking?

Nash's eyes flicked over the whole board, but Gerard sat immobile, his lowered eyelids and curved lips making him look rather sinister. She had seen that look before, but where? Ah, yes. General Soutine had regarded them that way when he'd seen them at the theater. Gerard must have mastered the trick of it from him. Nash would be able to read nothing from his face.

Nash finally moved and Gerard slid his knight out.

"Check," Gerard said so quietly she was not sure Nash had heard.

His uncle leaned back and scanned the board desperately.

She knew better than to break their concentration, but she had to. "Gerard, don't you think you should go change?"

"I already have."

"But that isn't the sort of coat Great-Uncle is used to seeing, not in the country at any rate."

"But it is *my* coat. Don't you find it fashionable? I'm pretty sure you saw me wearing it at the theater."

"I know, but really—"

Just then the other men entered and the dead silence that arrested them on the threshold was followed by an oath from General Cochran.

"What the devil are you wearing?"

"My trunk finally arrived," Gerard said brightly, getting up and turning so they could perceive his finery to the full.

Juliet could see Nash smiling. It made him look just a little like Gerard.

"And that was in it?" the general demanded as Charles gaped at their cousin.

"Yes, it was made by the best Parisian tailor." Gerard pulled out a lace handkerchief and fluttered it. Juliet clapped a hand to her mouth but was unable to prevent a squeak of surprise.

"Well, get rid of it. We'll go to Brigstock this afternoon to order you some proper clothes."

Gerard tilted his head and smoothed the front. "Perhaps it is too fancy for the country."

"Go change *now*."

"Oh, then I would miss the end of this very interesting game…and luncheon."

The general glanced at the board. "I cannot conceive how he got himself into such a fix. Nash will concede the game. He cannot possibly win. Go change now. The ladies are dawdling anyway."

Gerard went toward the stairs with a smirk on his face, and Juliet looked at Nash as though to ask him what insanity this was as the other men found seats in the drawing room.

"Don't look at me. I did warn him." He stared at the board again as though going over the sequence of play in his head.

"Shall we put the pieces away?" she asked.

"No, I mean to continue the game at least with myself."

"But he has you in check. I see no way out for you. Even Great-Uncle said it was hopeless."

"It's always a mistake to assume there is *no* way out. One of life's best lessons. In fact, Gerard has informed me there is a move that would result in a stalemate between us and a different move that might result in my winning."

Juliet studied the board again. "But what are they?"

"I would give much to know."

She nodded. "But would never ask him."

He looked up at her. "Of course not."

Then something occurred to her. "Are you sure he was talking about chess?"

For the first time in her life she left Nash looking stunned.

The meal was spent in relative calm, the ladies making lists of what they needed from town and the men discussing wool prices and the grain crop. The traveling carriage was called for as well as Chandler's phaeton, which could seat three. Jack disdained the shopping expedition, so there were only the nine of them going.

To keep peace Gerard agreed to the carriage, with Chandler conveying Melanthe and Juliet in his equipage. Claude made no objection. He would not get to sit next to Juliet, but neither would Gerard.

An hour later they alighted at the King's Arms and Claude went in to order some brandy. He looked back as though he expected his father to follow him, but Nash trailed after the other men while the ladies set out for the milliner's shop.

Whatever else he was, Nash had impeccable taste in fabric and style. The general said he would leave Gerard in his hands while he went to the express office. After visiting the tailor, the haberdasher, and the bootmaker, Gerard found himself back at the King's Arms sipping an ale and watching his grandfather beat the dickens out of Claude at piquet.

The general had engaged a private parlor and ordered tea for when the ladies returned. Gerard noticed he had trouble reading the suits of the cards. How frustrating that must be for him. No wonder he asked Chandler to write his letters. Of course he could employ a quizzing glass or even spectacles, but that would seem like a sign of weakness.

Just as the laughing group of women entered laden with packages, the coachman came and rapped on the door with a grave look.

"What is it?" General Cochran asked.

"One of the team has pulled a shoe. We may have to leave it to be shod and hire another horse in its place."

"Has it lost it or loosened it?" Gerard asked.

"Loosened, but it is sure to come away on the trip home."

"I'll have a look," Gerard said.

The general glared at him. "What do you mean by that?"

"One of the many useless skills I acquired during my travels with the army was emergency farrier work." Gerard rose and followed the coachman to the stable.

"My grandson, shoeing horses?" he sputtered, causing Gerard to pause and look back at the family.

Claude looked outraged and Nash worried. Helen's face was livid.

"Oh, no, sir. The claimant to that title is going to shoe a horse. When my identity is proved, I'm sure I'll get too high in the instep to even think of touching a horse's hoof."

Chandler chuckled and got blasted by a violent glare from the general for his lack of restraint. While the ladies had tea, the gentlemen trooped to the blacksmith shop and forge next door, but as they had been informed, the smith was not working that day.

Gerard liberated the tools he needed, removed his coat, tied on the leather apron, then went back to the stable to pull the last nail out of the loose shoe. He rasped the foot even and set the shoe back in place. As he tapped the new nails in and clenched them he said, "A cold-set shoe isn't as good, of course, but I imagine it will hold until it's time to have him shod."

"Did you learn anything else in the army?" Claude gibed.

Gerard put the hoof down and removed the leather apron with a smile. "To always pay for what I take. Our absent smith deserves something for the use of his tools and the nails I liberated." As Gerard walked away he fished in his watch pocket for a coin. Without turning his head he said, "I also learned how to keep my mouth shut."

The coachman had a coughing attack but Chandler laughed outright. Gerard glanced at his grandfather and saw that slight smile that made him look so much like his father. Even Nash had a rueful look.

"Shall we take the ladies home?" General Cochran asked.

"It won't hold," Claude shouted as the coachman led the horse out to the carriage. "Lay you a monkey it doesn't hold."

Gerard looked around in time to see Nash clap Claude on the back and whisper something furious into his ear.

Juliet noticed that Claude looked mutinous on the drive home. Gerard perched on the back of the phaeton, where a tiger would ride, behind Melanthe and Charles to watch the leader he had shod and call a warning if anything should go amiss. She had taken the seat between her great-uncle and Nash, leaving Claude to be flanked by Helen and Emma opposite them. Claude had a bad habit of sitting with his knees akimbo and crushing the skirts of any lady sitting next to him, so she had scrambled to get the seat opposite him.

He mumbled about the upstart until his grandmother elbowed him in the ribs. Helen had looked elated when she'd learned of Gerard's *faux pas* with the puce coat but was now chagrined that he had helped the expedition— or rather that the general had accepted his help. Yet worse, he had called him his grandson, a severe blow to their campaign to unseat Gerard. That besides General Cochran having committed to buying Gerard an expensive wardrobe. Helen probably thought her husband would pay those bills, but Juliet was just as sure Gerard would pay out of his own pocket.

They arrived too late to change, so dinner was a hurried affair and the evening in the drawing room promised to be an uncomfortable one at best. And then what must Gerard do but produce a flute, which he unfortunately could play. He suggested Juliet accompany him on the pianoforte. To her relief, he could read music. Jack volunteered to turn the pages of sheet music for them. Many of the pieces she knew were not at all suitable for a flute, but if the notes went below his range he booted them up a register. It amazed her that he could transpose in his head. They had some laughable starts and stops, but really it was an enjoyably informal evening, and it was not just the two of them laughing. General Cochran guffawed and Nash even cracked a smile once or twice when she looked up. Only Claude worried her. He sat drinking. The more his grandmother glared at him, the more persistently he drank.

After a time, Gerard asked Jack if he was able to get a sound out of the instrument and when the boy did, he gave him some pointers right there in the drawing room. He was teaching Jack music in front of his grandfather and not being reprimanded.

Finally Gerard declared himself exhausted and put a period to the entertainment, but when he reached for a cigar and made for the door, Juliet slipped into the hall after him.

"Do not get caught alone out there with Claude."

"I shall evade him. My army upbringing will finally

be of some use." He walked to the back door, picked up the lantern, then stopped and asked, "Has he ever threatened or hurt you?"

She smiled as she walked up the stairs. "You are not the only one skilled at evasion."

The light had faded by the time Gerard reached Tully with the tale of the loose shoe and the offer of more smokes. He added the reactions of the family and made the old man chuckle even more.

"I knew I should have insisted on coming," Tully said. "That must have been something. The grooms are in awe of you. I doubt any of them would be able to shoe a horse."

"Necessity makes for some strange skills. What do you think? Shall I stay here if I manage to prove up my claim?"

Tully delayed as he lit up, then clenched the cigar between his teeth. "How could there be any difficulty? I could vouch for you if you think that would serve."

"And reveal yourself? If the general knew you were Father's batman he might send you packing. At least three of the family want me to be declared an impostor and I'm not so sure I want to be part of this clan."

"Wot about the fair Juliet?"

"She might marry me even if I am an impoverished medical student."

"She won't be allowed."

"That's the rub. I fear without me about she may lose courage and give in to their wishes."

"If you stay, you'll be master here someday and can do as you please."

"You mean be tied to the place for the rest of my days. I'm not sure I want that. What do you recall of

General Soutine?"

To Gerard's surprise, Tully looked nonplussed as though he had never expected the question.

"Wot did your father tell you of him?"

"Nothing."

"Then there was nothing he wanted you to know. I reckon him to be a kinder man than I had ever thought, to have saved your life. Why did you come to the battlefield anyway? I thought you safe in Brussels."

"I asked for news as I dealt with the wounded. That last day it seemed so grim. Then soldiers from our unit started coming in, all badly wounded. I had to know."

"I was separated from him," Tully said. "A shell exploded nearby. I was wounded but tried to get to him. I could not even find him. Then I passed out. When I woke it was the next day and I was in Brussels. But I hitched a ride back out and spent the next few days looking for him."

For the first time Gerard realized that he had decreased Tully's chance of survival by picking up that drum. If he had stayed in Brussels he could have taken care of Tully and searched for his father himself. "Why was Soutine looking for my father?"

Tully scratched the scar on his cheek, looking uncomfortable and blew out a breath of cigar smoke. "Do you believe in keeping promises?"

"Of course."

"Even to the dead?"

"Are we talking about Father?"

"Yes."

Gerard clapped his old friend on the shoulder. "Keep your promises. I can find out on my own. I never like it when things are too easy."

Juliet had gone upstairs, but only for a dark cloak, and she was making her way to the stable when an arm reached out and grabbed her. She squeaked and barely avoided a kiss from Claude, who reeked of brandy fumes. She kicked and struggled, but he now had each wrist in a vise-like grip and was forcing her arms apart so he could get at her face.

A *thwack* dropped him on top of her, but Gerard soon rolled him off her and pulled her free.

"What did you hit him with?"

"A piece of firewood. I would have made it a fair fight but I wanted to stop him now. Are you all right?"

"Yes. Do you suppose you've killed him?" she asked breathlessly.

Gerard bent to check the beat of Claude's heart.

"Worse luck. He yet lives. What shall we do with him?"

"This is no laughing matter, Gerard. If you had killed Claude, we would be in the suds. Besides, sometimes I feel sorry for him."

He stood up. "Why?"

"He hasn't had the benefit of Great-Uncle's mentoring the way Charles has. He was raised by a wet-nurse and Helen and is still under her thumb."

"I had thought Nash would be more of an influence."

"Not when Claude was little. I don't know if anyone can repair that damage."

"Shall we leave him here to sleep it off?" He reached for her arm and she let him take it.

"And hope that he cannot remember what happened?" she asked.

"Seems a bit heartless even after his attack on you.

Sober, I hope he would not have treated you so."

"I have always been able to fend him off with my threats to tell Charles. I hate to resort to that."

"You should not have to threaten him to assure your safety. I'll walk you back, then report Claude drunk on the lawn. No, I will get someone else to do it so no blame attaches to me."

"Sometimes I think you are too clever by far. That will get you in trouble someday."

"*Someday?* It gets me in trouble all the time now."

They arrived at the back door and Gerard took her hand to examine her wrist. "He has bruised you."

"I will wear gloves."

"Why hide his abuse if this has happened before?"

"Because it's embarrassing. I should be able to manage on my own."

"Not to be able to handle that brute. No, the victim should not be embarrassed. She should be outraged."

"But if I accuse him I would have to explain what I was doing out here. He would say I led him on, or worse, was coming to meet you."

Gerard pursed his lips. "But you were coming to meet me."

"I was not." She felt her heart hammering against her chest as he stared at her in concern.

"What are you doing out here?"

"Looking for you to warn you that Claude had come after you. But they would think the worst."

"So we can hide our attraction or have them think the worst of us."

"I suppose it comes to that."

"If they are going to think ill of us, we should at least enjoy this moment." He bent his head and kissed her, gently at first, then more boldly as she did not resist but kissed him back. He pulled back to stare at her and run the tips of the fingers of one hand over her lips, which trembled at his touch.

"We should go back in," she whispered.

"I remember you kissing me awake in the carriage when we got to Calais. It felt like an upside-down fairy tale, a lost frog being awakened by a princess."

"Let us not end up like two characters in some Shakespearean tragedy. Let us do whatever we must to be together."

"What if Grandfather disowns me?"

"I will elope with you."

He chuckled. "And here I was thinking you might lose courage. You are braver by far than me."

"Still, we should go in before we are discovered." She moved past him, but he reached for her and slid his hand along her arm until their fingers came together in a strong clasp.

"We should. One more kiss, since we've had so few. If it pleases you, will you marry me?" He kissed her and held her tenderly against him as though he was afraid she would flee.

"What a very strange proposal."

"I love you dearly, but I want you to be happy so much I would give you up if there is likely to be a better future for you."

"I want no other future than to be your wife."

"Even if I am cast out like my father?"

"I will go with you anywhere. It may be difficult. My fortune is not my own for many years."

"Then I will become a blacksmith in London and you will play pianoforte at the opera."

"Now, why didn't I think of that solution? We have to remember we are not helpless but can work for our keep."

They finally ended their embrace and went in, Juliet running up the stairs while Gerard hunted up two footmen to help Claude back into the house. He hushed it up as best he could, though Nash saw them bring him in through the back door.

"What the devil?" Nash asked on his way through the hall.

"The grounds are treacherous at night," Gerard informed him. "It's as black as the belly of a whale out there."

"No doubt." Nash turned to the footmen. "Take him to his room. His valet Grimpel will see to him."

Chapter Nine

The next morning it poured, so Gerard did not expect any interruption to his drumming lesson for Jack, but they had to cut it short when Juliet ran down the stairs to warn them that the general and Chandler had left the estate office to work in the library and were asking for him.

When Gerard wandered in, they had a large map rolled out on the table. Nash was there looking over the map as though seeing it for the first time.

"Gerard, did you hear gunfire?" the general asked.

He shrugged. "Uh, thunder perhaps?"

"Never mind. This is the layout of Old Stand along with the lands we have acquired. Two hundred and forty acres altogether."

"The wool mill isn't here?"

"No, that's in Northhampton where there is enough labor to support it," Chandler said.

"This is the grist mill." Nash pointed to a building between the road and the river. "The only one within ten miles, so it does quite a business at harvest time."

"Pennies compared to the wool trade," Chandler added.

"At least it is constant income. Whereas if the sheep get wool maggot or the fleeces rot, your losses are bigger too."

"This isn't a competition," the general warned them.

"Is this the stud farm?" Gerard pointed to an area of the map.

"Yes, small." Chandler pointed to buildings east of the long drive. "It doesn't make any money. Not like the cattle or flocks." He indicated the cattle barns and fields to the west of the drive and the sheep sheds to the north on top of the hill.

"Or the mill," Nash added. "All the newly acquired land to the east is used to grow grain. How does it feel to have it all laid out before you?"

Sadly, it reminded Gerard of his father's battle maps, and he wondered what had happened to them. "This is neither a war nor a game but serious business. One small mistake could ruin all. I shall make very sure I am never at fault in breaking it all to pieces."

That brought a strange light to his grandfather's eyes. "No one will have any say in it while I yet live. Certainly it will not be broken up."

Gerard felt himself smiling. "Then all is safe for a time, a very long time, I hope."

"Do you indeed, Cuz?" Nash asked.

Gerard smirked at Nash's use of the familiarity, then thought of something. "Where is Claude?"

Nash sent him a measuring look. "He has a headache this morning."

****

After luncheon, the rain slacked off to a drizzle, but Juliet was surprised when the general called for the carriage to visit the sheep close. On the way, their great-uncle listened as Charles delivered a lecture on breeds and wool, nodding his approval. Juliet was the only lady interested enough to accompany them. Pride in her brother's knowledge must have shone in her face. Claude came with them but appeared to have a hangover. If he noticed a lump on his head he said nothing.

"This is mostly short rough staple wool," Gerard said. "Have you thought of expanding into merino or some of the other soft staple wools?"

Chandler nodded. "We would love to, but the breeding stock is hard to come by."

"I've seen merinos in France. I just can't recall where." He did remember the scent of the sheep, rich in lanolin and sweat. They did not remind him of the battlefields of Europe but of someplace more peaceful and of his mother. As he watched the white lambs bouncing and chasing around the fields at Old Stand he thought of a field bordered by yew trees and suspected it was part of that elusive estate he remembered. The memory was so fleeting he might have imagined it. Certainly he must have imagined the peacefulness.

"Let me know," Chandler said. "It may be possible to import breeding stock now."

"If I can place it. Where to now?"

"The cow barns in this weather would be a worse quagmire than the sheepfold," General Cochran said. "Let's go to the mill."

"Did you build the mill or buy it?" Gerard asked as they piled into the carriage.

"Bought it and rebuilt it," Nash said.

Gerard was impressed that his grandfather did not mind interruptions from his heirs but seemed to assess their knowledge and perhaps even show a bit of pride in them, however outspoken they were. Gerard realized he had a lot to learn and he would only learn when he was listening and asking questions.

They took the lane that led downhill through the

sheep pastures, then onto the drive and across the road to the mill. When they arrived, an old man limped out to talk to the coachman and help with the horses. He spoke with an accent, possibly Prussian. Gerard hopped out after the others to discover a lady miller with a touch of accent to match the old man's. Her hair was done up under a kerchief and her smile was entrancing. She was a sturdy woman, of about forty, with a flat yet beautiful face. She smiled at sight of them, especially Claude, and invited them into the first floor, which served as delivery room and office. Juliet stared at her open-mouthed and Gerard kept her from saying anything by pinching her elbow as the general introduced him to Anna Herrick.

"Sorry for the noise, but we got a load of grain to grind today," Anna said.

"Is this the first of the harvest?" Nash asked.

"Yes, we all hope for a better harvest than the last two years, when we had barely enough to feed the livestock and make bread."

"Summers have been cold and wet, "Claude said. "We may lose much of what grew to rust or mildew."

"The winters and springs have been harsh as well," Nash conceded. "If the weather would cooperate, we could run the mill round the clock."

"And you could afford to hire more than Da and me to run the place," Anna replied.

The general smiled. "No one has ever complained of your management, Miss Herrick."

"Da can still work, but his hearing is not so good. Hazard of the job, I suppose."

"I hear a gear that needs grease," Claude said, tilting his head to one side.

"Da meant to get to it, but he doesn't get about as

good as he used to."

"Where's the grease bucket?" Claude asked. "I'll be able to figure out where it is."

Chandler looked impatient, so Gerard said. "I'll go with Claude."

As they climbed the ladder up a story to where the grain went into the grinding hopper, Gerard wondered how greasing a gear could be an acceptable task for a gentleman whereas shoeing a horse wasn't. It could only be that no one would see Claude flaunting his humble expertise. Unerringly Claude identified the noisiest gear of the mechanism and globbed grease on it from the bucket he had brought. Gerard risked a look out the window at the moving mill wheel and the water race below. The spray of water from the paddle wheel bathed his face in a cool mist, but the noise storm made him feel dizzy.

Someone grabbed him by the shoulder and his heart almost stopped, but Claude dragged him back in rather than pushing him to his death.

"The stonework is all wet from the rain. It would be easy to slip and fall."

"I see that now. You seem to know a lot about mills. So much more complex than the wool trade."

"Anna was my nurse when I was little, so I spent a deal of time here with her and her Da. As her father got older and I grew up, it seemed the best thing for me to help out here. Kept me out of trouble."

"I see. Because they did not need to hire someone to maintain it, the Herricks were able to stay."

"I suppose you could say that. Grandfather doesn't see everything. If you tell him he needs a manager here, they would be retired. And what else are they to do?"

"I think your arrangement makes sense and is admirable." Gerard smiled, for the resemblance between Claude and Miss Herrick's Da was noticeable. Perhaps she took care of him because he was her little brother. It never occurred to Gerard to say anything about his suspicion. After Juliet's initial recognition of the resemblance, he hoped she would be as discreet.

Claude had been accepted by Nash and the family. He was Nash's son in all ways that mattered. But something about Gerard's suspicion did not seem quite right. He could not reconcile in his own mind the prudish lady in the portrait with a woman who would commit adultery with the local miller. Aside from the age difference, how could they have ever managed it? And then there was Claude's slight resemblance to Nash about the mouth...

As they went back down, the grinding continued with a reverberation that shook the floor, but the squeaking had stopped and Claude beamed triumphantly.

"You found it," Nash said.

"Yes, no problem."

"Perhaps we do need more help here," Chandler said as he looked at the grain sacks, then at the feeble old man.

"There's little enough to keep one miller busy," Anna said.

"We need a good harvest," Nash added.

Gerard was glad that Juliet had not said anything, though she had realized there was a connection between Claude and the Herricks. If no one else had put it together, all was well. Or he could be wrong, Gerard thought. One thing war had taught him was never to assume anything.

On the way back, they stopped at the stud farm. The mares and foals were out grazing and the stallion locked up. Gerard saw at least one colt who had the look of Wagram and wondered if the beast had escaped at some point and visited the mares' field. He also wondered if Tully would be content to work here. The more he thought about Old Stand and Juliet, the more he wanted to stay. But he knew the fortunes of war applied to civilian life. A thousand things could go wrong with his plan. He wasn't even sure he had a workable plan yet.

Before they got back in the carriage, the general pointed out the wooded slopes running along the west side of the estate to the upper pastures. "We sold a deal of timber during the war."

"So that's what Old Stand really means."

"Yes, the old stand of timber planted two hundred years ago. What did you think it meant?"

"In my mind I *had* given it a military connotation, a place where a stand had been made."

"You would."

"Is any of the old stand left?"

"In spite of supplying masts for the navy, we have preserved enough oak in case any of the major beams in the house, mill or barns require replacement."

"I am used to complex plans, but they are all executed within a few days or weeks. Here you must plan for generations."

"You see now why the succession is so important?"

"Yes, but it is a job for more than one man. Old Stand must never be divided up."

"I agree."

"Perhaps that's why Father wanted me to study law, to find a way to hold it together."

His grandfather arched an eyebrow at him. "Or a way to get your hands on it."

Gerard felt shocked and at a loss for words when he realized General Cochran was not joking this time. "We can never know. But I know my father, and he would never have countenanced such a thing."

His grandfather sent him a measuring look but did not reply.

Juliet realized that a carriage full of women coping with an expedition in the rain might be peeved, whereas the men returning to the house looked to be smiling in good fellowship. One should never underestimate the male comradeship to be got from tramping around in manure of various kinds and poking about a noisy mill.

She had to admit she seldom went inside the mill because the floors all shook and gave her shivers. The building seemed alive, like a giant machine that could swallow her up. That's why she had never met Anna before. Clearly Gerard saw Claude's resemblance to the Herricks as well. There could be two explanations for that. And she juggled them back and forth in her mind as they entered the house and shook the rain off their coats.

Gerard and Claude were joking with each other on their way up to change for dinner. Perhaps they had made their peace and Claude would give up the idea of marrying her. Maybe the Cochrans could all run the various business interests of Old Stand together in peace.

Later she saw Helen's forbidding face and realized that their struggle was far from over. Even if Gerard managed to charm Nash and Claude, the latter was too easily manipulated by Helen. She would start something again. Depend on it.

It happened over dinner.

"If you do not plan to marry Claude, who will you marry?" Helen asked.

Juliet stared at her a full minute. "I have decided not to marry. It solves everything."

Melanthe looked alarmed. "But what will you do with your life?"

"Study. I have been neglecting my music. Perhaps I will become a piano virtuoso and play for the opera house in London."

Gerard chose that moment to choke on a bite of bread, and Chandler helpfully pounded him on the back, which must have hurt his ribs. Her brother was an idiot.

The stunned silence was relieved by Nash's chuckle. "Our dear cousin is having you on, Mother. She has no intention of playing at the opera in London." His smile twisted uncertainly. "You don't, do you?"

"Not at present. But who knows what exigencies I might be pushed to by demands to know my immediate plans?"

The general gave an uncertain laugh. "Yes, I think we all agreed not to discuss such matters at table."

To Gerard's surprise, the agenda that evening included dancing. Of course Juliet would have to play unless they wanted no more accompaniment than his flute.

When Claude danced with Melanthe or even his Aunt Emma, he had a grace that Gerard had not expected in a big man. Perhaps he lost his self-consciousness then, as he had at the mill, climbing sure-footedly up the ladder to grease the gear.

Gerard had made the mistake of thinking him a slow top just because he was sturdy and not much like any of the Cochrans. But it took some thinking to remember the steps of the country dances, and he was far from perfect himself.

As they finally sat down to tea, they were all smiling for once. When Claude smiled he resembled Nash, at least about the mouth. Gerard sighed. All that business of thinking Claude illegitimate was nonsense. He did look like a Cochran, a little. Then Gerard choked on a sip, for he thought of another explanation for Claude's resemblance to old Herrick. He did not know how they had managed it, but Claude must be Anna Herrick's son and Nash's. In some ways that possibility seemed even more unlikely than what he had thought before. As he coughed on his tea, he decided it was a good thing he had not spoken of his suspicions, though he had no such intention even now. Certainly what he was thinking would get him tossed out the door. Somehow he had managed to salve Nash's ire up to a point. He would just have to win Claude over. *How* was the puzzle.

His mission had changed in his own mind since he had thrown himself between Chandler and a ball of lead. First it had been to save his cousin's life, not so much to get anything out of it but because he liked him and would have hated for Juliet to be bereft. Then it had been to stay close to Juliet to fathom his attraction for her. He was in love with her, probably had been since he had first seen her. But romantic love was a new emotion for him, so he had not recognized it at first.

Ingratiating himself with his odd family had been for fun and, he had to admit, to spite Nash and Claude. Now he was determined to keep them in the fold. The only member of the family he could not imagine making peace with was Helen, but that might not be necessary. If Chandler continued to handle the wool trade, Claude could be the one who kept the mill running. And Nash? Perhaps Nash could be the one to write letters for the general.

They were all looking at him in concern and he realized he'd been staring into space. It was premature of him to be planning anyone's fate. He was not in charge and never would be if Helen had anything to say in the matter. How much hold she had on his grandfather he did not know.

A commotion sounded in the hall, and Gerard realized Jack was drumming the charge. What's more, so did the general whose hawklike glare turned toward him. That would put paid to any rapport he had built with his grandfather. He glanced at Juliet and she sent him a speaking look, accusing him of putting Jack up to this. Gerard shook his head. General Cochran strode to the doors and flung them open. Jack seemed delighted. He marched in with the drumming steady as a watch and entertained them with several more orders while his grandfather scowled at him. Gerard could not but be proud of the lad's courage, though his initiative was sadly misapplied.

Jack's mother Emma was glaring at Gerard by the time the drill finally ended, and then General Cochran did something strange for a man who was disenchanted with the military life. Instead of blasting the boy, he walked back and forth in front of him as though Jack was on review. Finally he spoke. "Your drumming is not so ill, but you look like a scrubby schoolboy out of uniform. And if you tell me learning this skill has convinced you to join up, I will lock you in the dungeon from which you unearthed this instrument, and keep you there until you are too old."

"Oh, no. This was just for fun. Besides, the war is over."

The general bent over and spoke into Jack's face. "And just what was this display in aid of?"

"Everyone is always saying how stupid I am or that I'm too young to ride a horse or do anything exciting. I just wanted you to see that I could learn something all on my own. Well, I had a bit of help."

"An effective demonstration, if ill-timed." The general stood up straight and smiled indulgently. "What do you want to become? I hope not a traveling player."

"Oh, no. I want to become a surgeon like Cousin Gerard."

General Cochran's gaze drilled through Gerard as neatly as a bullet. "I see. Dismissed," he almost shouted. Jack marched out and so too did the rest of the family, not quite as smartly but willingly, to escape the storm that would break over Gerard.

Gerard tossed off the rest of his tea and stood up. He exited last and asked, "Your office?"

He could hear the breath the general expelled. "Yes, I want to discuss your penchant for meddling and your future, probably at more length than you would like."

Gerard was standing more or less at attention in front of the desk when General Cochran finally came in the door and closed it.

"Oh, sit down. This is not a court-martial. Though if I thought you had put Jack up to this performance I would throw you out of the house tonight."

"It was him playing with the drum that led me to the basement. When he asked how you drummed the signals, I showed him, and one thing led to another."

"I see." Once again Gerard had the feeling that his

grandfather saw more than he said or even more than Gerard did.

"I have no right to interfere with the boy, but it worries me that someone told him he was too stupid to do anything."

"If you are asking who that was, I don't know, and it worries me as well. First I had Nash to deal with. Now he seems to have pulled himself together. But Claude is the current problem in the household. If Jack goes in the same direction, I don't know what I will do. And it took a newcomer to point this out to me."

"Jack simply wants attention and companionship. I find it a mite odd that he would turn to a complete stranger for that."

"Nevertheless, if you encourage him in this ambition to become a doctor, or hold to it yourself, you can depart. Only the original holding of Old Stand is entailed to the heir. I can leave the rest of it as I please."

"I am happy to hear that. But you speak as though proving my identity is a mere formality."

The general gave a bark of laughter. "You are too much like your father in every way, including your misapplied sense of wit, to be anyone else. What will it be?"

"My inheritance or my freedom? I would regret having to choose."

"You would live to regret it when you are living in poverty."

"I would regret it because I would miss all of you— well, perhaps not all of you. But even Nash has proved an interesting acquaintance and I do not despair of coming to terms with Claude, given time."

His grandfather stared at him in disbelief. "Now you

are boasting. Even your father could not stomach Nash, and Helen has made Claude impossible."

"People can choose to change their lives."

"But not their natures. You would give up everything, including Juliet?"

"Juliet has vowed to marry me, but I would let her out of that promise."

"You do work fast and covertly. Rest assured that proving yourself will mean nothing to me after tonight."

Gerard's sudden smile seemed to confuse his grandfather. "But at least we understand one another."

"No, Gerard, I do not understand you at all. You're far too sensible for someone your age."

"Must have been the war." He was turning to go when a rap came on the door. He hoped it was not Chandler coming to rescue him again.

When Gerard opened the door, a footman came in. "An express rider, sir." And carried the old man a message. General Cochran said nothing, just took it. Gerard left the room closing the doors carefully behind him.

When he got to the landing, he discovered Juliet sitting on the striped settee, looking out the window into the dark. He stopped a few steps up and stared at her. How could he not choose Juliet? Suddenly his future burst upon him like a branching tree, not a crossroads. He could wait to fulfill his destiny later. Juliet needed him here and now.

She looked at him and made an effort to still the trembling of her hands. "You are in the suds now," she said. "The general thinks you have been corrupting Jack."

He came and sat down upon the bench beside her.

"Yes, the boy's timing could not have been worse. General Cochran informs me that the study of medicine, especially surgery, is not a gentlemanly pursuit, and if I insist upon it I can take myself off."

"Would you throw all this away to prove a point?"

"To be my own person? Eventually I may have to. You see, I have always taken orders. Now I know what I want to do."

"Always? You were not taking orders when you followed your father into battle."

Gerard smiled tiredly. "I always tried to take orders. Perhaps I should go back to Soutine. This was supposed to be just a visit."

Juliet felt herself on the point of tears. "Is that why Soutine has such a hold on you? You were used to taking orders?"

"I am as puzzled as anyone else by my reaction to Soutine. He's old, alone, and in pain. It was while staying with him that I finally decided to go into medicine."

"If you turn your back on your family, you may end up the same as him."

Gerard reached for her hands and took them between his own. "I love you, Juliet, but it would kill me to stay here as a mere dependent. I must have some employment. I wanted to study medicine even if the only way I could afford to do it was on a battlefield."

"How ironic," she said, looking up at him. "In keeping you from following your dream, your grandfather may drive you into the army just as he did your father."

"No, he will never be able to make me do anything I don't want. I just hope the price for staying does not become more than I can afford to pay."

"No matter." She held her chin up. "I am coming with you."

"What? I do not ask that of you."

"No, I'm coming with you whenever you leave here, whether it be years from now or tonight."

"I know you are a woman of rare courage, but it's not fair for me to ask you to give up everything because of my goal, a goal I can easily put off for a few years."

She leaned toward him and kissed him, her eyes almost crossing in her effort to take in all of his face.

He looked puzzled. "I wonder if this is much like the choice my mother made."

"Of course not. There is no war now."

"For the moment. We are all safe for now." He helped her to her feet and released her hands.

As they walked up the remaining stairs to the second floor, she asked, "What was all that choking about?"

"I thought you meant to announce I would support you in London with my blacksmithing skills."

She laughed. "No, I mean later, during tea."

"Oh, nothing."

"You never do anything for nothing."

He stopped at the door to her room. "I cannot tell you just yet, but I have to venture out tomorrow. What would be the closest village in the parish beyond Sudborough and Brigstock but a place the family would not frequent?"

"Grafton Underwood is the next closest, but there is no direct road. The fast way to get there is to go to Brigstock and backtrack."

"I mean to go by back lanes and find it. Do you want to go?"

"I should not."

"We can take Jack and Tully for propriety."

"Or my maid," she whispered.

He chuckled. "Let's say we mean to take her and then forget."

"I know. She turns queasy at the very mention of a carriage ride."

He looked puzzled. "Why did your hire her?"

"I didn't. Helen did."

"And you are too kind to dismiss her."

"I suppose. But what are you looking for?"

"I cannot tell you, for I may not succeed in my quest. I may be wrong. I'm sorry. Trust me that it is necessary."

She nodded with the realization she would trust Gerard with her very life. The door had closed behind her by the time she remembered she had not discussed with him Claude's resemblance to the Herricks. But Gerard obviously did not want it spoken of, so she would not. It would not seem fair anyway to use something against Claude that was not his fault.

Chapter Ten

The next morning Juliet was pleased that Gerard let her takes the reins again. Admittedly they were on back roads with no traffic, and it was a one-horse gig, but it felt good to know she could drive a horse as well as ride one. It was to be Jack's turn on the way home. He was squeezed in between them on the single seat, radiating excitement. She expressed concern about Tully riding so far, but Gerard laughed at her worry and assured her they had traveled much farther in one hour on campaign, and usually on foot.

Since all the participants in the expedition were early risers, and all but Tully normally met in the box room in the morning, escaping without notice or permission was not difficult. It did occur to Juliet that they probably should have taken a groom who knew the country better than Tully, but Jack was handy at asking directions, and they reached Grafton Underwood before most of the household would even be out of bed.

Gerard left Juliet and Jack to order breakfast at an inn while he went on his errand. By the time he got back, Jack was tucking into sausages and toast while Juliet poured tea.

"I should not be eating with quality," Tully said as he sipped his ale.

"It's a tiny inn, Mr. Tully," Juliet said. "You would be eating in the same room anyway, so you may as well sit at our table."

"She's right, Tully. Besides, Juliet informed me the family never come here."

"And why have we come here?" Jack asked after swallowing a huge bite.

"To visit the church."

"Church? It's too early." Jack's dark eyes lit with curiosity. "Why did you really come?"

"I am not at liberty to say, except that my errand has been successful," Gerard said with a satisfied smile.

"Does that mean you'll be allowed to stay at Old Stand?" the boy asked.

"No, Jack, it does not, but I plan to stay if I am allowed."

"I'm sorry if what I did makes the general cast you off. I thought he'd be proud."

"He was proud of you, Jack, but I had no right to teach you without at least your mother's permission."

"She is fit to be tied. Says I'm not to consort with you ever again."

Tully laughed. "So this don't count as consorting, boy?"

"No, we are not conspiring for me to learn more music. Besides, by what Mum says, Gerard is to be cashiered out."

"What does that mean?" Juliet asked.

Gerard smiled. "Turned off, drummed out, whatever you like."

"I suppose I had better pack," Juliet said, causing Tully to raise his eyebrows.

"Don't be so hasty. Perhaps the lawyer will approve my claim, or perhaps the uncertainty will drag on for a while. There are worse things than waiting."

She stared at him a moment and realized that for a couple to be married without a license they had to post the bans three weeks in a row. She was not of age, of course, but they could lie about that. If Charles could be convinced to sign for her, though he was not her guardian, and no one raised an objection, they could be married in that amount of time. The alternate requirement was that they reside in the same district for fifteen days, but it came to the same thing. Could Gerard last two more weeks at Old Stand? It would be interesting to see if he could manage their escape better than the one Charles had arranged for him.

In spite of Jack driving and Gerard suppressing the boy's notion to spring the horse, they beat the rain home. When Jack drove the gig up to the house, Gerard took the reins from his hands. Gordon immediately came out as though he had been on watch for them.

"Where have you all been? The general thought you had eloped."

Gerard laughed. "That's absurd. Would we take a scruffy schoolboy and no baggage if we planned to run away?"

"I did not think so, but they never listen to me. The express last night was from the London solicitor, Mayhew. He is to arrive this morning."

"It's nearly noon now. And has he?"

"No, but I was afraid he might before you got back. Frankly, as far as I know, Jack was not even missed."

"Yay!"

The boy hopped out and scooted around the corner of the house—to sneak in the back door, Gerard supposed. Tully tied his horse to the back of the gig and drove it off toward the stable, and Gerard took Juliet's arm to lead her in to luncheon. "Perfect timing."

"Where the devil were you?" General Cochran demanded as they filled plates at the sideboard.

"Driving lesson," Gerard said, then pulled out a chair for Juliet.

Even Chandler glared at him. "If Juliet wants to learn to drive, I think I am more qualified to teach her."

"Oh, no. She was teaching me."

Chandler looked aghast, and Gerard then remembered that he had claimed to be able to handle a team of six, so he laughed at the stunned-ox look on his cousin's face. The general merely shook his head and went back to eating.

Gerard looked around the table, winked at Jack, but noticed no one was smiling, plus there was an empty chair. "Where is Claude?"

"He had an errand," Helen said.

Gerard suspected it had something to do with the news of the solicitor coming. Before they had finished eating, the skies opened, but he dodged another chess lesson by claiming to have letters to write. He did actually compose a letter to General Soutine, a humorous account of his stay to date that would leave the old man chuckling. He pointedly did not ask the meaning of the contents of the trunk. Two could play at that game. And he dangled the same temptation in front of Soutine that he had in the previous letter. It would be interesting to see if the old man could resist.

After that Gerard sprawled on his bed reading one of the French novels Soutine had tucked into his trunk, a lurid piece full of pirates and abductions. Perhaps this was some reference to his hasty exit from France.

A sharp rap came at his door.

When he opened it Juliet stood there, looking so vulnerable and uncertain he wanted to take her in his arms.

"Let me in."

"That I shall not. It would be insane."

"I must speak to you in private."

"Come out onto the balcony over the portico."

"But it's raining sheets." She pulled her shawl about her.

"There is a roof." He opened the door, checked the hall, and slipped out with her. "What is so important that you would risk your reputation?"

"Jack told me someone galloped out of the stable yard right after we got back. From the man's size, he thinks it was Claude."

"I see." He had to raise his voice to be heard above the rain.

"Do you think it has to do with the express the general received?"

"Yes, and if the London solicitor is late, Claude might get back before him. But what can be his errand?"

"Helen has arranged for you to be examined by the York solicitor as well. But General Cochran says he will not delay the hearing."

"Ah, the York man is in Helen's pocket. How do you know this?"

"My maid babbles from time to time, so she is some use. Be prepared to be doubted."

"It is good to be forewarned, but I can hardly stop Claude riding like a maniac for York. He will either return before the London man gets here or he will not. I doubt he will be able to bring Helen's man in time."

"Anyone who looks at you would know you for a

Cochran. Even Charles bears some of the Cochran features through our mother, the chin anyway, and the smile. Not so much the eyes and eyebrows."

"Certainly he is not inclined to our lean build."

"No. Nor is Claude. One would not take him for a Cochran at all."

Gerard shrugged. "He has Nash's smile."

"Hard to tell. Neither of them smile very much."

"He has been accepted as Nash's son, and that will never change, should never change."

She looked at him a moment. "I agree."

Gerard had his back to the rain and was pretty much soaked but had managed to shield Juliet from most of the spatter. He took her in his arms and kissed her reverently.

"What was that for?"

"Agreeing with me. You should go in now. The wind is chill."

"What was it like, sleeping rough?"

"We seldom did. My father was an officer. If there were any quarters to be had, we slept under a roof. Perhaps a leaky roof," he said as a trickle of water ran down his neck from the old gutter. "But a roof all the same."

"You said the only way you might be able to afford an education was in the army."

"Only as a last resort, if I am driven away from here."

"You're not leaving without me?"

"Not willingly."

"I will come with you."

He kissed her again. "But it would be better if we married and left the normal way. There is no need to panic yet. Now, to get you safely back to your room."

"I'll go first," she said.

"Check the hallway," he whispered.

Helen's noxious voice berating Juliet for opening the balcony door sent Gerard by means of the ailing gutter up onto the roof above.

Fortunately the house was only two stories at this point, with the servants' attic surrounded by a wide expanse of slates—slippery slates. Gerard heard someone close and lock the balcony doors and knew it was incumbent on him to get back to his room before it occurred to Helen to check for him there.

He crept along the edge of the roof on his knees 'til he judged he had come to his window, then swung down beside it on the guttering using his right arm to take his weight.

A tentative attempt to raise the window with one hand revealed that it was locked. He wadded his handkerchief about his left hand and punched the pane next to the catch. The tinkle of glass brought Gordon to open it.

"What the devil?" he asked as he helped Gerard scramble in.

"Be a good man and forget how I entered."

"Certainly, sir. But if it is one of the housemaids, I will leave your employ."

"No it is Miss Chandler, but we have done nothing wrong except converse on the balcony," he whispered as he climbed over the sill.

"In this rain? Meeting like that is very dangerous."

"If I get caught alone with her, they may try to force her into marrying Claude."

"I appreciate the difficulty, sir, but that is not the only danger. You might have been killed." Gordon stared down at the flagstones below, then drew the drapes over the broken window pane.

"Only if I had fallen. And it's no more than twenty feet. I have fallen farther than that."

"Indeed?"

Gerard did not elaborate but stripped off his wet coat and shirt and thrust them at Gordon, then reached for his dressing gown and shrugged into it with Gordon's help, just as Helen and Nash thrust the door open.

"I say, have a care. I might have been naked."

"Have you been in here all this time?" Nash asked.

"I've been reading a dull book. What is the matter?"

"He must have come in this door when I went to get you," Helen said.

"Gordon," Nash said. "Did Gerard just come in?"

"He did not just come in that door, and no one should open it without knocking," Gordon said stiffly. "Especially a lady."

Gerard turned his gasp of laughter into a cough. "What is the matter?"

"Apparently nothing," Nash said as his gaze wandered to the slight blowing of the draperies.

Helen went away grumbling and Gordon carried Gerard's wet clothes into the dressing room. Gerard turned toward his bed where he had left the novel, but Nash clamped a commanding hand on his right shoulder so hard it jerked him to a standstill.

"Listen to me, boy. I may concede that Juliet would not make the best wife for Claude. She is by far too managing. But I have a grudging regard for the young lady. If you do anything to destroy her reputation, you will meet me for it, and I won't be teaching you a lesson. It will be for real."

"Thank you, Nash. I had no idea you thought so well of Juliet."

"She is possibly the most normal one among us. Have a care what you do, or at least don't get caught."

"I would never hurt her, and I do hope to marry her if no rub is thrown in the way. But I can hardly court her in public."

"No, Helen would intervene. What about Chandler?"

"I have his permission to make addresses to her."

"But not for an elopement. That's what everyone thought you had done today."

"Except you. What made you believe in me?"

Nash folded his arms and regarded him. "The way you play chess. It kills you to give up so much as a pawn, and you never risk your queen."

Gerard stared at him in amazement. "Even though she is the most powerful piece on the board. I promise you I will never carry Juliet into danger or ruin her reputation. I am trusting you not to tell either Helen or Grandfather that she is the only person holding me here."

"The only person? What about Jack?"

"'Tis true I see in him myself not so many years ago. He needs someone's attention in place of a father, but I am not the person to take him in hand. He regards me as too much of an equal."

"You mean a cohort. Surely you are not suggesting I should take on training him."

"You have to give me lessons in being a gentleman. What harm is there to including Jack?"

Nash groaned. "Very well. I will speak to Grandfather about the boy."

"And Juliet?"

"I'm not a snitch." He glanced at Gerard's hand. "You might want to get Gordon to bandage those knuckles."

He left then and Gerard wrapped his bloody hand in a handkerchief as he puzzled over why Nash would do so much for him, until he remembered rescuing Claude from the lawn. Something else had seemed too familiar about the situation. Then he realized it was Nash's voice. When not sneering or gloating he sounded a bit like Gerard's father. Perhaps Gerard had more than two reasons to stay.

****

Juliet had not changed her story about checking on the guttering, though she doubted Helen believed her. The way her maid was sniffing about the room, she half suspected Sophie of tattling on her. Such a bother. The girl was never about when she was wanted but always seemed to be spying on her when Juliet wanted to do something clandestine like meet with Gerard. Or perhaps it was just guilt.

But she did not think she felt at all guilty about her fiancé. She was walled up here against her will—just like Charles, when he could have managed the affairs of both of them. Of course his actions in France might have got them in the suds if not for the quick thinking of Gerard. Already she trusted him more than she did her impulsive brother.

She would never give Gerard away. But how to support him in his coming trial she had no idea. What if the York solicitor had managed to forge some documents that would disinherit him? As she changed her damp clothes, she thought about the promises they had made to each other and realized that even if Gerard was cast out they still had a future. Charles would find enough money to send Gerard to school and help them live 'til she came into her own. Her brother liked Gerard.

There would be a scandal, of course, when they ran away to Grafton Underwood to marry, but once the marriage was consummated she did not think either Charles or Great-Uncle would push for an annulment. She did not think about what she and Gerard would do after that. She had always saved her pin money and must have almost a hundred pounds hidden about her room. As soon as she could get rid of her maid, she would gather it up and pack a bag that she could grab at a moment's notice. She must also write a note for Charles in anticipation of their escape.

Dinner was a tense affair that evening. Though they waited all day for the London solicitor, he did not appear. Helen gave no explanation for the continued absence of Claude, though General Cochran did ask where he was, as they all filed into the drawing room after the meal.

"We have enough for two tables of cards," the general said, "If everyone will play."

"Not me," Emma said, "I mean to sew."

Juliet smiled. "I should like to watch Nash and Gerard play chess. Perhaps I will learn something."

Nash looked aghast at her suggestion. Obviously he had not resolved the unfinished game from before.

"Too bad we do not have a second board," Gerard said as he set the pieces in their starting positions. "I fancy it's a game Jack would enjoy, and four of us could play a tournament."

"There is another set," the general said. "I will get it while the servants arrange the tables."

When he came back and opened the small leather

case, Gerard recognized it at once and could not suppress an intake of breath. "That is Father's chess set. How did it get back here?"

"Are you certain?"

"I lost one of the pawns and had to carve a replacement. It took me days."

Gerard watched the general tumble the pieces out of the sack and picked up the pawn, cruder than the rest and held it in his hand. Perhaps that's why he always identified with the pawn—he had been one too often. Even now he was not free, but it was because of Juliet. It was his choice to stay and win her. He would never win anything by running away.

The general took the piece and set it on the board. "It was in his trunk when it was returned."

Helen gasped. "That should not have been got out until the lawyers are present."

"Lawyers? Plural?" he queried.

"Of course I sent for my solicitor. He is the one with the interests of Nash and Claude at heart."

"This is not a trial but an inquiry," he reminded her.

"And you have stacked the evidence in his favor." She pointed at Gerard as she left the room, supposedly in tears.

In the end, no one played cards but sat and watched the chess matches and participated by turns, except Emma and Melanthe, who were sewing. They were frosty to Gerard because of the incident with Jack. It was a quiet evening but one of intense concentration. Charles had the style Gerard expected, reckless and flamboyant. Against any of the careful Cochrans he never won a game.

When matched against his grandfather, Gerard felt

almost as though he was playing his father at chess, and it occurred to him that the old man must have taught his father to play. Another connection with the past.

General Cochran flicked his gaze around the board. "How does my playing compare with General Soutine's?"

Gerard considered well before answering. "He will sacrifice any piece to win, including the queen."

"He was like that on the battlefield."

"The chess board is his only battlefield now. I wonder if Napoleon ever played chess."

"Only on a very large board," his grandfather said. "What made you think of him?"

"Because you play more like Wellington would. Every sacrifice you make is well considered, and when your opponent stymies your plan, you 'tie a knot and move on.' "

"What do you mean?"

"You amend your strategy on the fly, and if your opponent does not fall into every trap you set, it does not fluster you. Soutine plans too far ahead. That is the flaw both he and Napoleon share."

"And did you fall into his traps?"

"Only to find out what his grand plan was."

General Cochran chuckled. "Why do you like chess so much?"

"Because it's just a game. It doesn't matter."

The intense gaze bore into him. "Nothing is just a game. Everything matters."

Gerard nodded and lost to his grandfather as gracefully as he always had to his father.

Jack started to model his play after those who won by patient teasing of their opponents with small sacrifices and the setting of traps to which his agile mind quickly tumbled.

Juliet also set traps and made some brave sacrifices. She usually won, more because her opponents underestimated her than because she cared about the game. Gerard had the notion she was studying them, all of them. To her it was a game within a game. If he married her his career as a pawn might continue the rest of his life, but he did not mind at all.

Chapter Eleven

Everyone was up early the next morning expecting the solicitors to arrive, so Nash took the opportunity to call Gerard and Jack into the library to instruct them in gentlemanly behavior. Since this involved introductions to ladies, Juliet was called to their aid. Because even Jack took the exercise quite seriously, Nash did not get frustrated.

Gerard had borrowed books from the library but had never spent much time there, his grandfather preferring to conduct business in the smaller estate office at the back corner of the house that looked out on the stable yard. Midmorning, the sound of a carriage drew them all to the front window except Nash.

"Is it the custom for well-heeled gentlemen or even ladies to be peering out the window for company, or should they simply wait for the servants to announce the arrival?" Nash asked.

Jack laughed. "You got us there, Cousin Nash. I should not tell you who it is, just for that."

Gerard took Juliet's arm and conducted her back to her chair. "The London man, I take it. No doubt he left yesterday and was detained by the weather, probably put up in Northampton. The timing would be right."

"York is much farther," Nash said. "Probably Father will meet with Mayhew in his study until luncheon. Let us begin the whist lesson, if we can play on this table.

Since you did so well at chess, Jack, I think you could become a terror at cards."

After another hour a footman came to remind them it was time to eat.

Over luncheon Gerard had a chance to size up Mayhew. He seemed jovial and in good accord with the general. So why did his grandfather think this whole business necessary? The answer was obvious once he thought about it. If the solicitors accepted Gerard, then Helen and Claude would have to shut up about him. A week ago he would have included Nash in that number, but somehow his uncle had come over to their camp and Gerard was glad for it.

When it was obvious everyone was finished eating, General Cochran rose and instructed them all to go to the library.

"The whole family should be present," Helen insisted. "We must wait for Claude to return."

"That I shall not. He knew better than to go off on a start when there is family business to be conducted."

They entered the library to find a circle of chairs surrounding the large table, on which a trunk sat unopened. Gerard would have recognized it as his father's even had he not seen the initials stamped into the leather. A flurry of hooves on the drive drew them, including General Cochran, to look out the window, which made Nash groan and look heavenward in despair. A post chaise and four stopped in front of the house and unloaded Claude and a black-clad man with a large portfolio under his arm and a pair of pince-nez perched on his beaky nose.

"Your solicitor? Damn, woman. He looks like a jackanapes."

"He is here to protect my interests."

Mayhew raised his brows but said, "So long as he does not interfere, I have no objection to his presence." He did seem to take offense, though, when the other solicitor pulled a chair up to the table and cleared his throat as though he meant to take charge. "I am Roth from the firm of…"

"Stop," the general said. "Your presence is at the discretion of Mister Mayhew. If you cause any disruption or speak out of turn, I will toss you out the door myself."

Having paid the post boys, Claude came in and took a seat near Helen. She smiled at him but it did nothing to lighten his scowl over a sleepless night and probably other difficulties. Still, Gerard was impressed that Claude had pulled it off, a man of action after all.

"This examination is to determine the identity of the applicant, whether he is Gerard Cochran, son of Major John Cochran and grandson of General Alfred Cochran, or not." Mayhew stood. "The first two items are uniforms. Do you recall any distinguishing marks?" He looked toward Gerard.

"Father had three uniforms. I recall a saber cut on the sleeve of one that was repaired. The other two were worn but not damaged."

They pulled out the blue artillery officer's coat and examined it. "No saber cut," Roth said and made a note. It was laid on the table along with a second uniform, not the one he had worn at Waterloo, of course. That would have been buried with him. Gerard had no idea how much it would affect him to see these things, so dear yet so sad. He almost wanted to call a halt, tell them to close the trunk and he would give up any aspiration to replace his father.

Then he looked toward Juliet and her so-sympathetic eyes. Chandler nodded to him as if to say, *Go on.* Nash was looking lost, and Gerard wondered if the emotion of seeing his brother's things would overcome him. This was not what Gerard had been expecting, that Nash had loved his brother. It made him bite his lip and pull in a breath. He'd had months to get used to the idea. Though intellectually Nash knew his brother was dead, he had not really confronted the truth until now.

"The next item is a journal. Can you tell me what is in it?" Mayhew asked without lifting the journal into view.

"His notes on the battles. I was never allowed to read it. It's covered in scuffed brown leather. No monogram, and it has a lock."

"It is locked and there is no key."

"He would have carried that with him," Gerard said.

"Shall we break the lock?" Roth asked.

General Cochran's hand came down on the solicitor's. "What would be the point? Gerard has never seen the contents."

Roth cleared his throat. "The applicant claims wisely that he has never seen it."

"The next item is a box of playing cards," Mayhew continued, very much as though this was an auction.

"The box is wood and the cards well worn." Gerard could visualize the familiar items and they brought back a flood of memories—his mother and father playing late at night by lantern light, his mother teaching him whist and, after she had died, Tully teaching him the less refined games. "The backs have fleur-de-lis on them. They were a gift from my mother."

"They are as described," Mayhew said with a slight smile.

"But anyone might have seen these," Roth insisted.

"The next item is a chess set." Mayhew looked about and consulted the list again. "I don't see it."

The general cleared his throat. "We had need of the chess set last night, but Gerard properly identified it as his father's."

"That was unconscionable," Helen said.

"But a better test than this," General Cochran said. "He had no idea where the chess set was. It could have been one I had here."

"Is that it?" Gerard asked.

"There is a book."

"I do not recall a book. Unless it is a military volume he borrowed from someone, I cannot imagine what it could be."

"It is a book of poetry," Mayhew intoned.

"But that's absurd," Gerard said. "Father never read poetry. He called it rubbish."

"That is correct," General Cochran said. "I inserted the book of poetry as a test."

"But you don't read it, do you, sir?" Jack asked in some concern.

General Cochran's mouth quirked in a quick smile. "Of course not."

"That is all that was in the trunk?" Roth asked. "No papers?"

"Just some shirts, civilian coats and smallclothes," General Cochran answered. "Even if we had his saber that might not help, since there was nothing remarkable about it."

"No doubt lost in the battle," Mayhew replied.

The general sighed. "I suppose he may have stored military papers in the locked journal, his commission and such, but—"

"Since this person is in this country without leave, I think he should be turned over to the authorities," Roth said. "No passport for him has been found in the trunk."

"What the devil do you mean?" Cochran asked. "Military are exempt from the need for a passport."

Helen rose from her chair. "As you have said often enough, Gerard was not in the military. Chandler removed him from France illegally. I don't know who he bribed to let him into this country, but this person is French, not English. You can tell by his accent."

"Chandler, how did you get Gerard into the country?" General Cochran asked.

"The same way we got him out of France. We said we were taking home a relative wounded at Waterloo."

Juliet cleared her throat. "Besides, Gerard has his passport. My maid should keep you better informed, Aunt Helen."

Helen colored at this accusation and sat down.

"I'm only half French," Gerard mumbled. "But I can prove—"

"You cannot," Roth almost shouted. "You were born in France and should be sent back there."

Gerard removed a new bill case from his pocket and extracted a worn certificate he placed in Mayhew's hands. The solicitor smiled.

"This is a baptismal certificate from St. Thomas' Church in Portsmouth for Gerard Cochran, son of Major John Cochran and Mrs. Amilee Cochran."

Gerard pursed his lips so that he would not smile as everyone stared at him. Most of them wore looks of surprise. His grandfather's gaze spoke of vengeance at some future date for putting them all through this charade. Nash looked almost amused, Claude angry, and Helen murderous.

"You little devil," the general said. "If you had this all along, why did you not say so?"

"I thought someone might claim I'd stolen it."

"I did tell you he had papers," Chandler said. "Recall that I discovered Gerard in Paris quite by accident."

"But you went there to inquire for him?" Helen accused.

"Yes, but everyone who knew him thought he had either perished on the battlefield or gone home."

"The applicant may have put himself in your path," Roth insisted.

"Gerard was very reluctant even to come to meet his grandfather," Chandler replied. "In truth, I had to abduct him to get him out of the country."

Gerard glanced toward his grandfather and saw puzzlement on his brow. Later he would ask him why he had not wanted to come. Gerard was glad he had not brought out the money belt itself with that damning letter. He was convinced now that General Cochran had not written it and probably did not know its import since he could not see that well. If Gerard had his way, his grandfather would never know. For if he found out, he might think Gerard's father had believed it, and he sincerely hoped that had not been the case.

Into the lengthening silence Claude spoke. "Has he tried to escape since he has been here?"

"No, but he has fallen in love with Juliet," Chandler said with a smile.

So much for keeping their engagement secret.

"Yet another reason to maintain the imposture," Helen countered. "Besides, a baptismal certificate means nothing. If his parents were not married, he is not the legal heir."

Nash's head came up at this accusation and he looked at his mother as though he would like to throttle her.

"I have that as well." Gerard handed another much-creased paper to Mayhew.

General Cochran coughed to cover a chuckle. "Have you played your last card?"

"Almost," Gerard said as he saw the hint of a smile on his grandfather's face.

"This is a certificate of marriage for the couple in question. It's somewhat blotched, but there is no doubt about the signatures, and the date is clear enough."

"And when is it dated?" Roth asked.

'More than a year before the baptism."

"Enough," the general said. "I am satisfied that Gerard is my heir. This is finished."

Roth gestured wildly. "By his own mouth he speculated these documents might be stolen. In point of fact, he cannot produce a single witness to verify his identity."

General Cochran stood. "His face is his witness. No one can look upon Gerard and deny he is a Cochran."

Helen glared at Gerard. "He could as easily be another son, a bastard son."

"Mother!" Nash leaped up. "Don't say such things."

Juliet stood. "Actually he can produce a witness."

"What?" The men all chorused.

"Juliet, don't," Gerard said.

She turned to him. "But they don't believe you. Not all of them."

"Does it matter so much if I am proven Gerard or not? You said it didn't matter to you, and that's all I care about."

Juliet turned to her great-uncle. "Sir, does it matter to you if he can prove he is Gerard or not?"

"I believe him already, so does Chandler, and you, of course."

Helen tossed her vinaigrette down in disgust, breaking the bottle on the floor. "It matters to me that my son and grandson are going to have their inheritance stolen by this French scoundrel."

"I must tell them, Gerard, or she will never shut up about it. You can protect Tully if he is turned out."

"Tully?" Chandler asked. "Your groom?"

"Yes, he was Father's batman during the war. He had thought me dead and came back here hoping for word of me."

General Cochran started laughing and rang for a servant. "He's the one who brought the trunk."

When the butler entered, he said, "Send to the stable and have Tully come to the house. Make sure he hasn't been mucking a stall or something."

"What is so funny?" Helen demanded. "He could be an accomplice."

"It's just like Gerard to have a certainty and not reveal it. Come to think of it, one of his proofs of identity is his reprehensible sense of humor."

Tully appeared, dressed not in the good clothes he'd bought with Gerard's largess but in his worn batman's uniform. He had been expecting this. How? Juliet, of course. She never left anything to chance.

"General Cochran, sir." Tully clicked his heels together.

"Do you know this young man?"

"Gerard Cochran, sir. I've known him since he was a child."

"That's good enough for me," the general said.

"But how do we know Tully is who he says he is?" Roth demanded.

"I happen to have my military papers right here." He placed them on the table.

"Tully, I leave you to wrestle with the solicitors. I think I need a drink." The general turned at the door. "And Tully?"

"Aye, sir."

"Why didn't you come forward before?"

"I feared my reception, coming home without the major or his son."

Helen glared at Nash. "Do something. Say something."

Nash stood and extended his hand. "Welcome to the family, Gerard. Such as it is."

****

Juliet looked around the rose garden, so tame in the sun after such momentous doings in the library. Even though the afternoon was fair they did not ride. First there had been a conference mounted in the breakfast parlor between Helen, Claude, and Roth. The general, Chandler, and Nash later retreated to the estate office with Mayhew.

The other ladies went cutting roses accompanied only by Gerard and Jack, who wandered off toward the linden plantation to the east.

"I think they might have included you, since this all

has to do with you," Juliet said as she clipped a white rose.

"I've done enough for one day. Recall I'm still wounded."

"As though you regard that. Do you think Helen will dare bring any kind of legal action?"

"Not without Nash's support." Gerard held out the basket for her next clipping. "So fortunate he came over to our camp."

"And how exactly did that happen?" She had seen it herself, Nash's gradual thawing toward her beloved, and she had to believe it was Gerard's honesty and nothing else at all.

He shook his head. "I'm not sure, but I am thankful. Did you fire your maid?"

"I did try, but she begged so piteously that I agreed to give her another chance. She says Helen threatened to sack her if she didn't reveal what had happened in France."

"That has the ring of truth." Gerard glanced toward the other ladies. "How far may I take you without risking censure from Melanthe or Emma?"

"Neither of them would care if we walked as far as the lindens. We'd still be within sight."

"I was hoping for a screen of foliage so I could steal a kiss."

Juliet smiled. "Are you very unhappy that I warned Tully he might be called upon?"

"No, for I no longer fear any repercussions. For him."

She laughed. "What possible repercussions could there be? It looks as though everything will turn out fine."

"Except for those who held that a council of war. Even if I am declared the heir I have no power as yet, so I cannot offer them anything to assuage this defeat."

"Why should you?" She wandered toward the arbor as if by accident.

Gerard set the basket down on one of the rough benches inside. "It's a very old rule of war not to leave your enemy with nothing unless you can absolutely defeat him. It makes him very dangerous indeed." He glanced toward the ladies picking roses, then dipped his head toward Juliet.

"Or her," she said as their lips met.

A shot sounded a split second before Gerard felt a firebrand score his left shoulder. He dragged Juliet to the ground and covered her as best he could.

"My God, someone has shot you."

"It must have come from the plantation. As in France, it is only a scratch."

"That doesn't change the fact that someone is trying to kill you."

Disregarding the danger to themselves, both Melanthe and Emma were running in their direction, but Chandler reached them first, just as Gerard was helping Juliet to her feet.

"Juliet, are you hurt? There's blood all over your hand."

"It's Gerard's. How badly are you wounded?"

Chandler stripped off Gerard's coat and used Juliet's shawl to bind up his shoulder, which was scored across his shoulder blade.

Melanthe was fanning Emma on a bench as General Cochran limped toward them. How odd. Juliet had no idea he'd had a limp. He must conceal it well, better than his vision problem.

"Lucky I leaned over to—lucky I leaned over, or I would have got it in the head."

"Look what Jack found," Nash said, striding toward them. "It's still warm." He had the pistol in one hand and Jack was at his heels.

His mother shrieked. "You should not be playing with guns, Jack! You nearly killed Gerard."

"I didn't do it. I was running to catch the villain who fired it and I found the pistol."

Gerard shrugged, then grunted at the stab of pain. "Emma, I believe him. Jack doesn't lie."

"Did you recognize him, Jack?" Nash asked.

"I didn't see his face. He wore dark clothes. I thought he was a poacher."

Gordon was shocked to have Chandler and Nash shepherd Gerard up the stairs to his room. They shut Juliet out in the hall as Gordon examined the wound, and it angered her. She was good enough to bandage him in France. Why not here?

As she paced the upper hall she heard a groom ride out, probably sent for the doctor. And there was a storm breaking in the drawing room, no doubt over the heads of Helen and Claude.

****

Some time later, Chandler opened the door and motioned with his head. Juliet burst into the room to see Gerard up against a bank of pillows looking a trifle foxed.

"This is such a noisy house," Gerard said. "Is the general ringing a peal over Helen or Claude?"

"Both, I think, and my maid is having hysterics."

"Why is she upset?"

186

Chandler had left the door open and crossed to the bed. "Perhaps she feels guilty for gossiping about you."

Juliet was wringing her hands. "Charles, I now suspect she complied with their wishes for pay."

Gerard sighed. "And having gone that far thinks she may be an accessory?"

Chandler shook his head. "Hardly, but Helen is capable of lying to her."

"Yes, we must remember that," Juliet said. "I think Helen could lie straight-faced to anyone."

"And that puts me in mind of something I wanted to ask both of you," said Charles. "Do you really think Great-Uncle wrote that wicked letter even in anger?"

Gerard shook his head. "I think Helen wrote it, and he has no idea what it said. Perhaps my father meant to come back someday and discuss it with him."

"I am so glad you did not use it this morning." Juliet fluffed the pillows though they did not need it.

"Let us destroy it now," Gerard said. "It's done enough harm, to my thinking. I don't want anyone else to read it."

"Where is it?" Charles asked.

"My money belt. I got it out of my trunk to get the documents, then put it back in."

"Here is the belt, but it's empty—no money or anything," Charles said.

Gerard took it and looked for himself.

"Is the money missing?" Juliet asked.

"No, all that was left inside was the letter. Who on earth would want it?"

"I shall speak to my maid."

"No. She might still carry our concerns to Helen. Say nothing. Chandler, ask Gordon to assess the servants, if there are any that might be capable of such a thing."

"Or of shooting Gerard," Juliet added.

"At least we know it wasn't Nash," Charles said. "He was with me."

"I don't believe it was Claude either." Gerard said. "If he wanted to kill me, he could have done so at the mill. He passed up a chance to knock me into the wheel race. By nature he is not evil, but he gets goaded into acting badly."

Juliet shrugged. "And passes it on. But Nash never treated him that way. He was hardly here when Claude was a boy."

"It all comes back to Helen." Charles folded his arms. "Sometimes I think she can make him do anything."

Gerard shook his head. "Not murder."

"Perhaps he wasn't so desperate before. And he was drunk?" Juliet said.

"He did miss," Charles reminded them.

Gerard felt so left out, propped up in bed in his room, that he had Gordon dress him so he could go down and have dinner with the others. He laughed to himself on his careful way down the stairs. A week ago he had wanted nothing to do with these people.

They were all surprised to see him in the drawing room. "Where is Claude?"

"Why do you care?" Helen asked.

"We should all care." He didn't bother to sit but glanced toward Nash, who had been standing looking out the window in variance to his advice.

"I think I know. I will go look for him. Do not wait dinner."

They moved into the dining room then and were quiet while the first course was served. When his grandfather asked where Nash could possibly have gone, Gerard looked at him. "Not very far."

For some reason that upset Helen. If Gerard was right in his guesses, Helen knew Claude had gone to the mill. There was no doubt Anna was the gentler influence on his life.

"How do you know?" the general asked.

"I did not hear a horse ride out."

"Oh, the mill," General Cochran said. "Claude used to go there for comfort. Anna was his nurse when he was little."

Once again Helen glared at them.

"Yes, I could tell she has a tenderness for him," Juliet replied.

The old man nodded. "He will come back when he calms down."

Abruptly Helen got up and left the table without even pretending tears. Perhaps Claude might someday be reconciled to Gerard as the heir. Certainly things could be worse for Claude, but Helen would have presented the outcome to him in the most disadvantageous way. And to what purpose? She could not now change the way things were...unless Gerard was to die. So whether she meant to use Claude as a murderer or hire a killer to get rid of Gerard, she was the one to watch. Given the chance, he thought he might win Claude over—but not Helen. There could be no reconciliation there. So one of them must leave, and a husband would have to choose his wife, wouldn't he? That was a depressing thought.

Juliet played for them after dinner since Helen was not there to object. After an hour she closed the keyboard and turned to them.

"I do not know about the rest of you, but I will turn in early."

Chandler and General Cochran went straight from the drawing room to the estate office. As Gerard went up the stairs, he hesitated on the landing and swung the door open to the balcony. He went out with some hope Juliet would join him there, but it was dangerous. He heard the great front door open and feet upon the stairs, but he was not the only listener. A patter of shoes from above met Nash and Claude as they came up the steps.

"I am not drunk, Grimpel," Claude said, "so leave me be."

"But I must help you undress."

"Leave me alone, both of you." By the sounds of it, Gerard surmised Claude stomped up the stairs, went into his room, and slammed the door. The soft patter of Grimpel's feet followed, but Nash turned to go downstairs.

"Is he all right?" Gerard asked as he stepped back in off the balcony.

Nash hesitated. "Depends. Are you alone out there?"

"For once. Did you talk to him?"

"Yes, and so did Anna—Miss Herrick. He usually listens to her, but Claude sees this as some kind of personal failure."

"He has no control over it and neither do I."

"That isn't what he wants to hear right now."

"For the peace of the family I should leave, get that education I want so badly."

"I thought you had given up on that in order to win Juliet."

Gerard shrugged, then grimaced at the pain this

produced. "Yes, I realized that if I left I could not win. But just because I stay does not mean I will win, either."

"I did not think you a coward."

"What?"

"I thought it would take more than a bullet to dislodge you."

"Oh, the shooting. That isn't what worries me. Helen will tear this family apart."

Nash put out his hand and laid it gently on Gerard's uninjured shoulder. "She already has, Gerard."

Chapter Twelve

The weather began to clear the next day, but the fields were still wet. Gerard was in the box room listening to Jack play on his flute. He did not think they could be heard, and there was little else for him to do with his chest bound so tightly he could hardly breathe. Besides, the music might help him think of a solution where he got everything he wanted and everyone else got something. That sounded so selfish, but what he wanted was for the good of all, if only they could see it.

The door opened and Claude came in looking strangely intent. "We forgot a very important part of your education."

"What's that?"

"Swordplay," he hissed. Gerard realized he had been drinking this morning even though he had not been last night.

"You mean fencing?" Gerard got up and nodded to Jack. "Lesson over for today. Go upstairs."

"No, I won't leave you with him."

"Go now, Jack." Gerard was glad to see Jack scurry out the door and up the stairs. He could only hope he would bring help before it was too late.

Claude threw open a trunk Gerard had never investigated and turned with two military sabers in his hands. "No, I mean the real thing." He tossed one to Gerard who caught it with the thought that Claude was at least playing fair. He could have just attacked him. Suddenly the Claude who had such unexpected grace on the dance floor took a pose that only an expert fencer would use and he moved back and forth with the grace of an Adonis. As the blows began to rain on Gerard's inadequate defense, he wished he had applied himself more at the fencing salon, although he didn't think fencing skill would be much good against this onslaught. Each blow felt strong enough to shatter Gerard's forearm. So he started blocking Claude with furniture. Discarded chairs and crates shattered under the impacts of his cousin's blows.

Helen slipped into the room, probably hoping to witness his demise. She locked the door, then slid sideways toward the other entrance, perhaps thinking to cut off any retreat through the storage cellar.

Gerard's saber shattered in his hand, a fragment of the blade slicing his coat sleeve as it was impelled away. "Quarter," he said as he retreated behind a table. There was pounding on the hall door and a heavy shoulder heaved against it, possibly Chandler's.

Claude hesitated, breathing hard. "So I have beaten you."

"I concede the match."

"Kill him!" Helen whispered fiercely.

Claude turned on her. "Stop telling me what to do!"

"Someone must."

Then Nash appeared in the connecting door to the storage cellar. "Claude, I beg you to stop. It is enough."

"Is it?"

"Yes, come with me."

Claude looked lost, as though he had just realized what he'd done. "But after this I'm the one who will have to leave, not that upstart."

Gerard stepped forward. "No one has to leave."

"It isn't too late," Helen said, her eyes almost mad with desperation. "Kill him now. We'll say it's an accident."

"That you will not," Nash said. "Gerard is the heir. But even if he wasn't, I'd not stand by and see him murdered."

Finally the door gave way and Chandler rushed in, followed by the general, Jack, and Juliet, who scanned Gerard's face to see if he was all right.

Claude threw down the saber and stalked out.

"Nash, go after him. No one has to leave," Gerard said, trying to think of an explanation he could offer for the general destruction.

"What just happened here?" General Cochran demanded.

"An ill-conceived fencing lesson?" Gerard answered.

"Fencing? With military sabers?" He looked around at the devastation. "Looks more like a war."

"Stupid, stupid," Helen chanted as she gathered her skirts and left.

Nash had gone after Claude, so they would believe any story Gerard told them, and he was desperately trying to think of one that would bring them all out of it blameless.

"Are you all right?"

"Fine," Gerard said in spite of feeling the familiar stickiness of blood on his shoulder blade.

"Well, report to Gordon and have him make sure."

His side had held together, but he'd torn a few stitches from his back wound. Gordon tied everything together again and convinced Gerard to rest. He woke late in the afternoon. Even though he felt like a broken doll sewn back together several times over, he wanted to appear at dinner if for no other reason than to show he wasn't hurt by the day's adventure.

Also, there was deal of packing going on and he could not make out who was leaving. Then all tramping up and down the stairs ceased and he heard his grandfather shouting from below stairs. Against Gordon's advice, he dressed and went down. His grandfather came out of the library looking like thunder.

"Get in here now."

In the space of time it took him to cross the hallway Gerard went over in his mind all the things he might have done to cause upset and for once came up squeaky clean.

Chandler was there as well as Nash, but he looked hurt rather than angry. Helen and Claude both looked smug. Now what on earth could have happened to turn the tables on him in a few short hours?

"Sit down," his grandfather commanded. "I don't want you passing out on us."

Gerard glanced toward Chandler, and his stare was no help.

"I was going to send Claude to London to live since you two cannot seem to get along. Nash was to go with him. Then I am told about this planned elopement and I don't know what to do with you."

"Elopement?" Gerard asked. "What elopement?"

Nash advanced on him looking hurt and betrayed. "You meant to elope with Juliet, and after my warning?"

"But that's absurd. I would never consider such a thing. It would ruin her."

"So why does Juliet have a bag packed with a letter

to her brother?" the general asked.

"I don't know? What does the letter say?"

"I do not open other people's mail." General Cochran handed the missive to Chandler.

He read for a moment and shook his head. "'Tis true, this is a letter of goodbye. You planned to steal her away? I can hardly credit it."

"That is absurd. I planned to wait until she came of age no matter how long it took. Are you sure Juliet wrote that letter? We've had some confusion about such matters in the past." He looked at Helen when he said it and thought she looked puzzled. So she did not have the old letter. Then it must be Claude.

Chandler looked again at the note with a dent between his brows. "It looks like her writing."

"Oh, for God's sake! Go get Juliet," the general commanded.

Juliet had been plotting how to get into Gerard's room to nurse him. She arranged a bowl of flowers and had started across the hall when Chandler informed her she was wanted in the library. She left the flowers on the table on the landing, sensing from her brother's expression that they would not match the mood of the meeting.

The first thing she saw when she entered was her portmanteau opened on the desk, and she gasped. She felt positively invaded.

"Who stole my bag? I bet it was that wicked maid of mine."

"And a good thing too that she carried it to Helen," her great-uncle said. "Otherwise you would have been gone."

"Juliet, why would you assume I meant to carry you

off?" Gerard asked.

Gerard's expression of confusion surprised her. Was he pretending innocence? If so it was not well done of him, but she would have to cover for him. "I'm so sorry, Gerard. When I realized what you were planning, I wanted to be ready to leave at a moment's notice."

"Planning? For what?"

"To get away." Why was he being so dense? It was his plan.

"You are a clever woman, Juliet, to have worked out a plan on your own, but you have outwitted me. What made you think we had to flee?"

Juliet felt herself flush as she began to have grave doubts about what had seemed so obvious before. "They weren't going to let us get married, at least not right away, or let you study medicine. On our own we could do both those things."

Gerard rose stiffly and came to take her hand, smiling sadly. "I know we joked about living on our earnings, but it is not that easy. And it would have been wrong at your age."

"Of course we could have done it. I have almost a hundred pounds, unless my maid has stolen it from my valise. If you have even close to that much we could easily live for two years."

"Where did you get a hundred pounds?" Claude asked.

"I saved it from my pin money." She held her head up proudly.

Into the dead silence this statement produced, Claude laughed. "You must be a changeling. No Cochran or Chandler was ever able to save money."

The general chuckled at this and that pulled a

reluctant smile from Gerard. Claude had made a joke, sort of.

"If I had been so villainous as to elope with you, we would not have been able to marry legally for years, but I would not be a doctor by then. I might indeed have had to support you as a blacksmith and you would have been ruined."

"But I thought you meant to marry me in two weeks' time. Why else did you go to the church at Grafton Underwood if not to post our banns or else obtain a license?"

"But, Juliet. You are not of age. Had I attempted such a thing, the curate would have written to your brother and my grandfather and scotched the scheme. It isn't just wrong, it's illegal."

"I thought you might have…lied to the curate about my age." She looked at him hopefully. "No, I suppose not. You never lie about anything. But why did you go there?"

He looked pained as though she'd revealed something she should not. "Not for that."

"I think I can answer that question," Nash said. "To discover that a very foolish young man named Nash Cochran married the miller's daughter there many years ago."

"You what?" General Cochran asked, his gaze swinging in Nash's direction.

Nash nodded. "Mother had it annulled, of course."

Gerard glanced at Helen, who was fuming, then back at his cousin. "Nash, you were both of age. She could not have had it annulled. Your marriage to Anna Herrick was legal then and is still in force unless there was a divorce I don't know about."

"Then I'm a bastard?" Claude asked.

"No, Claude. You are Nash's son," Juliet said. "As Gerard pointed out, you have his smile when you choose to use it."

Claude swiped his brow. "But how can that be?"

Nash looked as though the earth had dropped from under his feet. "Then my marriage to Diana was bigamy. Thank God it was never consummated."

"Then I am a bastard," Claude concluded.

"Shut up, all of you," Helen commanded.

"No, Juliet is right. You are my son."

Juliet stepped toward Claude. "I had not seen Anna before, but when I visited her I realized what a strong resemblance there is between you two."

"You were born while I was away," Nash said. "Anna delivered you a few days before Diana died of consumption. I was not told of this by Helen, who conspired to take you into the household as my rightful son. She gave it out that my wife died in childbirth. No one except the maids had seen her for months, so Helen got away with it."

"Not consummated," Helen grumped. "Nash, you are a bigger fool than your son."

"The marriage was not even real. We should return her dowry to the family." General Cochran was shaking his head as though confused.

"Claude was raised here as Diana's son and mine by Anna acting as his nurse."

"So I am the changeling?" Claude said.

"You are just what you always were," Juliet said. "Nash is your father and Anna your mother. They are both alive. You should be glad."

"How could all this happen under my very nose?"

General Cochran asked.

"If I am legitimate, then I am the heir because Gerard's father was disinherited."

"What?" demanded the general.

"I have come by a letter that you may not recall."

"Claude, no!" Helen cried.

"You told me to do something. My man has found this in Gerard's room, proof that Grandfather disinherited John."

"Chandler, would you read the letter," the general asked wearily.

"No, I will not. It is hateful and Gerard wanted it destroyed."

"We all want it destroyed," Juliet said.

Nash took the missive and scanned it. "Sir, I cannot believe you ever wrote such things to a child of yours."

Finally the general grasped the paper and held it at arm's length. "I cannot read all of it but this is not my writing. It is Helen's."

"I did what was best for all of us," Helen said, backing toward the door. "I was the only one trying to hold this family together."

"By keeping my son from reconciling with me? By denying his wife and child shelter? I will keep this letter in case it is ever questioned why you are living alone in York and not permitted at Old Stand."

"You cannot divorce me." Her hand went to her throat as though her heart had been taxed too far.

"No, that would be too easy for you. You will stay married to me but be a wife in name only. Pack your things. You are the only one leaving today."

"This is all your fault, Claude." Helen opened the door and strode out.

Claude growled and left the room.

"My head is still reeling," the general said, "but now that I think back, I see the truth of all this. Nash, you must bring Anna to live at Old Stand."

"No, that I will not. I shall do what I intended when you died."

"What?"

"I will reaffirm my vows to her, which I have never broken. I would like to live at the mill house with her."

"Claude could manage the mill," Juliet offered. "Gerard says it's one thing he loves to do."

"But you won't shut us out?" Cochran asked. "You will still be part of the family?"

"If that is important to you, yes, we will visit nearly every day."

"This is a shock for Claude," Gerard said. "I had never meant for any of this to come out."

Nash shrugged. "Perhaps it's as well that it did. Secrets such as these fester with time. I must go speak to him." Nash left them and neglected to shut the door.

"As for you two," the general said—but an under groom ran into the room.

"Sir, Mr. Tully sends word that Mister Claude has taken Wagram."

"Oh, no!" Gerard strode to the door, unmindful of all the things that ached.

"I'm sure he won't hurt the horse," Charles said.

"But it may kill Claude." He launched himself after the groom, shouting, "Saddle me anything fast. We must stop him before he gets to the woods."

Five minutes later Gerard took off on Juliet's mare, having a care not to hurt her. She was fleet and agile. He followed the sound of Wagram's hoof beats and finally saw his erstwhile cousin struggling with the old stud near the clearing where his own discussion with the horse had taken place. But when Claude tried to avoid the tree by the trick Gerard had used, he pulled the horse down on top of himself. The unmistakable crack of bone breaking made Gerard flinch.

Wagram struggled up, shook himself, then trotted off with his head held high to keep from stepping on the reins. Then he scented the mare and came back to chuckle to her as Gerard made a running dismount.

Nash came running down the drive and got to Claude first. He must have been headed for the mill when he heard the commotion. He started to raise Claude's head.

"Wait," Gerard said as he knelt and ran his hands lightly over his cousin's limbs. "Wait 'til he wakes and tells us what his injuries are."

Tully rode up and Gerard shouted, "Go get a carriage or wagon so we can move him. Then send someone for the doctor." Tully nodded and was off.

"I heard something crack," Nash said.

"His leg." Gerard undid the button of his breeches at the knee and saw swelling. "At least it's the lower leg and only one bone, not the thigh. If the femoral artery got cut in a femur break, he'd be as good as dead."

"We need to cut the boot off."

"Not 'til we get to the house. It will form something of a brace to keep the bones from moving any more than they have."

Claude woke and moved his arm.

"What hurts, Claude, just your leg? What about you head or neck?" Gerard asked.

"Just the leg. Is it broken?"

"Slightly," Gerard said.

"Stop mincing words, Gerard. Is it broken or not?"

Nash chuckled. "He means 'yes but not badly.' Stay still now." Nash patted his shoulder.

"I'm such a fool. I'm the one who doesn't belong."

"I think your grandfather might disagree with you about that," Gerard advised as he used his neckcloth to bind a stout stick to the outside of the whole leg. He motioned for Nash to strip off his neckcloth as well.

"Grandmother told me if I obeyed her, everything would come right, and it hasn't. I think it was my valet who tried to shoot you. I smelled powder on his coat."

Gerard sighed. "Then Grimpel can escort Helen to York."

"You love Anna anyway, Claude. Now I will be able to acknowledge her as my wife."

"But the world still thinks I'm the son of the woman in the portrait."

Gerard wadded his coat as padding under Claude's neck and bound the second neckcloth about the branch. "All will be well, Claude. At least you are a Cochran."

"Yes, all we Cochrans make stupid mistakes." Nash felt his son's forehead and smiled at him.

Gerard looked up at Nash and smiled. "More than our share, it seems. Ah, here come Juliet and Chandler with a wagon. Far better than a carriage."

"I'm sorry for the mess," Claude said, "but Grandmother swore you were an impostor."

Nash looked thoughtful. "Come to think of it, that's what she told me. Why did I believe her?"

Claude sighed. "When Grimpel showed me that letter, I thought she'd got it wrong. All that writing about being disinherited."

Gerard touched his brow and it was not hot yet. "She probably has her own copy of that letter ready to pull out at Grandfather's death."

"She's manipulated all of us for years," Nash said. "If I had not been grieving over my lost life, I might have realized it."

The head groom had arrived by then, and the men used blankets as slings to load Claude onto the wagon on a bed of hay. Gerard got up beside him to steady the leg, and Juliet knelt to hold up his head. Claude bore all with gritted teeth and no audible complaint. Nash grabbed a horse and rode to get Anna.

Juliet took a tray of broth and tea up to Claude's room, which was crowded with family. She should have let a servant do it, but Claude had been through a rough enough time, losing both his valet and his grandmother, plus the disillusionment he had suffered. The carriage had just left with those two, Helen's dresser, and Juliet's unfaithful maid. Juliet rapped on the door with the toe of her shoe and Chandler opened it. Anna was standing by the bed bathing Claude's forehead.

The doctor was packing up his bandaging materials. "Good thinking not to move the leg. It should heal fine in a few months, though you may get the occasional twinge."

"When the wind is in the east," Gerard said.

Claude gave a tired chuckle and accepted the cup of broth from Juliet.

"We should leave you to rest," Chandler said.

"I will watch over him," Anna replied. "I cannot believe it. After all these years, the three of us will be together."

Juliet hugged her. "I wish I had always known you."

Nash went to open the door for them. "I'll stay with him too. Gordon promised to help as well, though he is stretched a bit thin with all the recent *accidents*."

"I wonder what the servants think of all this," General Cochran said.

Nash shrugged. "The worst of our secrets have been exposed. Frankly, I do not care what they think. Before Gerard came, I was waiting for you to die so I could get on with my life with Anna. Now I find you accept her. I had only to tell the truth and our lives need not have been led in secret."

"The truth was ever a powerful weapon," the old man said. "I had forgotten that."

Juliet heard wheels outside and ran to the window. "It's almost dark, but I see a carriage coming up the drive with a team of four. I wonder who it is? Sorry, Nash, I couldn't help myself."

"Oh that's probably General Soutine," Gerard said. He went to stand beside Juliet and gaze down at the equipage, then turned to his grandfather. "In all the excitement, I forgot to tell you."

"What?" General Cochran asked. "You invited him here?"

"I'm surprised he accepted."

"You little blackguard. What am I supposed to do?"

"Receive him with hospitality as you would any old enemy."

"Very well, since I do owe him for saving your wretched neck, though I sometimes regret that. I'll tell Goff to prepare a chamber for him. I know. We'll put him in your father's room."

"The ground floor might be better."

"Oh, very well. Chandler, tell Goff to move my

things upstairs somewhere and put the general in my chamber."

Charles stared at his great-uncle as though he had run mad and left shaking his head.

Gerard took Juliet's arm as they came out the front of the house with General Cochran. When Condé had difficulty helping Soutine out of the carriage, they went to lend a hand. But someone else got out and helped the general. Gerard blinked and staggered. It was his father. He ran to him and almost bowled them both over when he clasped them each in a hug.

"Have a care, boy," his father chided. "You'll topple us all."

"But where have you been all this time, with us thinking you dead?"

"Nearly dead and out of my senses most of the time. I took a head wound and the locals must have picked my pockets before some enterprising Belgian farm wife carried me home in a wheelbarrow and nursed me back to health."

Gerard looked at him and noted the cropped hair and a fresh angry scar tracing a path along the side of his head.

"John, home at last," General Cochran said. "Left it a bit late."

"I wasn't sure I'd be welcome."

The general came and embraced his son. "Nonsense. I have been asking you to return for years."

"Really? I got no such letters."

The general nodded and looked at his son. "Letters do have a way of going astray."

"I am getting old, too old for this jaunting about," Soutine said, "and certainly for such heart-wrenching reunions in the middle of the road."

"We are all getting old, Soutine," General Cochran said. "Come inside, if you think you can make it."

"Nothing would dissuade me at this point. Has this young jackanapes been turning your household upside down?"

Gerard took Soutine's right arm as Condé grabbed his left.

"Yes, just as you foresaw that he would, but when the pieces all landed, we discovered we are still a whole family. By the way, this is Juliet Chandler, engaged to be married to Gerard."

"Congratulations. Ah, how sweet to be young."

"Gerard, you have been busy," his father said.

"After we found the major, we had to come," Soutine said. "I hope you do not mind we kept his life as a surprise. There is still one piece to the puzzle up in the air."

Having said that, he retired to his room, General Cochran's ground floor chamber, and did not emerge again, seeing no one but Condé.

"What is this revelation he plans to make?" Major Cochran asked his son as he poured himself a brandy in the drawing room."

"I had hoped you knew," Gerard replied.

The door cracked open and Nash entered. "Is it true? My God! John, you are alive!"

When his father and uncle came together the embrace was so genuine that Gerard no longer doubted the love between them.

"Don't ever do this to us again," Nash chided.

The general poured his youngest son a drink. "I always suspected you were fearing you would inherit,

Nash, and not living in expectation of it."

"Yes, when I have not the least aptitude for sheep or wool."

"Oh, as though I have?" the major said.

The general smiled. "On a place this big there will be employment for all."

"But how is this possible?" Nash asked.

His brother smiled. "Soutine kept searching for me and sending Condé to look where he could not go. I fancy he spent a great deal of money trying to find my remains. Instead he found me. If he had not come to me himself and recalled my memories of Amilee and Gerard, I'm not sure I ever would have remembered. And the farm wife had no incentive to remind me I was a British officer. I became quite handy in the dairy. Did I always know how to milk a cow?"

His father laughed and choked on his brandy. "No, that was never one of your skills. You become more valuable as we speak."

"The missing piece must be the connection between Soutine and Father. I know there is one," Gerard said.

Chandler poured himself a brandy. "He mentioned a debt of honor. Gerard doesn't know what he was talking about either."

"There is no mystery about that," the general said. "John married General Soutine's only daughter."

John swirled the brandy in his glass and stared at the amber liquid. "Yes, Amilee. I thought he would never forgive me for taking her off to war. But he's different now."

"So, that's it? Mother was his daughter. That's why he cared so much about me."

"And about me. We're all he has left."

"General Soutine is your grandfather as well," Nash said. "How wonderful."

"So that is the debt," Chandler said. "You took Amilee but gave him Gerard."

General Soutine entered at that moment. Juliet went to lead him into the room and find him a chair, though Condé had to help him.

"Not much good comes of war. I think we can all agree on that, but I am relieved to restore them to their home in spite of all they have lost. Is that brandy? I am permitted by my doctor to have a tot, just one."

Gerard moved to comply with his request. "Yes we have lost much, though Mother is what I miss the most, but I do have a family. For that I must thank you, though you went at it in a roundabout fashion."

"It was all up to General Cochran. I had hoped he had mellowed with the years as I have and put away anger and thoughts of vengeance. I see I am right."

General Cochran smiled. "A great deal of my reformation you can lay at Gerard's door."

"Mine as well." Soutine smiled at Gerard. "But if you had sent him back to me, if you had not accepted him, Gerard would have become my heir, not yours. Well, I have made him my heir anyway."

"Heir to what?" Gerard asked blankly.

The major laughed. "Have you been thinking that squalid lodging in Paris is all he has?"

"It's not squalid, but since I went back over to the royalists before this last battle, my chateau was restored to me with sheep, horses, cattle, and a hedge maze."

Gerard felt his jaw drop. "A hedge maze where a young mother played with her son."

"While she recuperated from a fever," Soutine said,

"just before her husband, an Englishman, came to reclaim her and their son."

"I still blame myself for her death," John said.

"No, you needed them with you," Soutine said. "You were a family."

"I often ask myself if Amilee would have lived longer at your estate than with the army train."

Soutine leaned back in his chair. "Impossible to say. But she loved you and would have been desolate without you."

"I have two grandfathers, then, to berate me. My cup runneth over, I think."

"If only John had brought you here before," General Cochran said. "I begged him to send you home, in letter after letter."

All faces turned toward him.

"I know," he said. "There never were any letters. Helen wrote them but never sent them. She has answered for her treachery in this."

General Soutine sighed. "Let us dwell no more on the past but discuss the future. Since Gerard will be my heir as well as yours, what is he to do for now?"

"I'm not sure. What do you think of his ambition to become a surgeon?"

"I think it's a crack-brained idea," Soutine said.

"On that we can agree."

Juliet looked from one to the other. "But it's what he wants above all things."

Gerard took her hand. "Not above all things, but it is what I am suited for with my war experience. What if Chandler helps manage the French holding? I fancy that is where I saw the merino sheep. Father can help with Old Stand except for the mill and grain fields, which must fall to Claude and Nash, who are the only ones who understand that business. Though I would like to see such a mill built in France as well. Father and Tully might be able to focus on the stud farm they were planning. Now that Father is back, I see no obstacle to my loping off to school, that is, if Juliet doesn't mind living in London for a while."

John laughed. "Give them an inch. I never heard a general divide up the work so neatly, but we are not yet ready to hand over the reins, so go to your school, whichever one you chose, but you must make a round of visits several times a year."

"And we may marry now?" Juliet asked.

"Don't ask me," said Chandler.

"Nor I." Soutine smiled at them.

The major nodded. "I see no impediment."

Juliet clasped Gerard's hands.

General Cochran nodded. "Then you have my blessing as well."

Gerard smiled and took Juliet in his arms, sure at last that they would never be parted no matter where their paths led, sure that her courage would carry them through any emergency where his might falter, and sure that his most important job was loving her.

A word about the author...

Barbara Jean Miller has mentored in the Writing Popular Fiction Masters Program at Seton Hill University since its inception in 1999. She writes in several genres but her favorite is historical romantic suspense. She calls them action/adventure romances with the heroine sharing in the struggles and rescue in equal parts with the hero. These struggles often involve mysteries and horses.

Barb lives with her husband and pets on an ancient farm in Western Pennsylvania, which contributes authentic settings to her novels.

https://barbarajeanmiller.substack.com

Thank you for purchasing
this publication of The Wild Rose Press, Inc.

For questions or more information
contact us at
info@thewildrosepress.com.

The Wild Rose Press, Inc.